IT TAKES A
MOTHER
a novel based on true events

Carolyn A. Vance

IT TAKES A MOTHER

first edition published 2020 by Simpleself-realization.blog
www.simpleself-realization.blog

ISBN 978-1-71693-891-7

Library of Congress control number: 2020907314

To those who seek truth, the omission is clear.

Disrespect for the mothers gives all the world fear.

It shatters our children, destroys our relations,

Weakens resolve; sets up war among nations.

1

Silvia was eleven when an extraordinary message floated like ether into her attention. It wasn't conveyed in voices like those that came to Joan of Arc. Yet it was crystal clear. *Help end racism.*

Inspired by *Wonder Woman* comic books and activist parents, she was already a warrior for justice. Her anti-racism outrage was fueled by a powerful empathy, as if she'd once been a slave herself. Anyone – child or adult – that used the 'N' word in her presence was subjected to a scathing lecture pointing out their confusion.

With her mission confirmed, a growing sense of purpose accelerated her maturity. She began to wonder about who it was that gave her this mission. The message had to be divine coming as it had. Maybe an angel had spoken to her.

Silvia wasn't particularly religious; at least not in a church-going way. Her parents didn't like the denominations they grew up with – Methodist for father and Catholic for mother – yet they agreed there was a Great Spirit who ran the show called life. And they wanted the community of like-minded friends that went with membership in a church. At the beginning of their marriage, they set out to find a faith that better fit their beliefs as well as their personalities.

Their research was still under way when their four children came into the world. Silvia, the second born, attended Sunday school with Presbyterians, Quakers, and Lutherans and Saturday school with Jews. Ultimately her parents declared the Unitarian Church the winner because its only dogma was that every member was responsible for seeking truth.

This church remained the chosen one after Silvia's marriage to her high school sweetheart, Frank Nolan, and the births of their beloved children. They liked the kids' Sunday school because it explored nature's miracles and the wisdom of all of the well-known religions. But Silvia and Frank seldom attended regular Sunday services. Frank preferred playing golf as the way to uplift himself, while for Silvia, it was in the church meeting rooms filled with kindred souls fighting racism that made her feel in league with God.

It was an intense era for the fight, and Silvia recognized that no matter how difficult the struggle, she was lucky to have been born into such a time. Dr. Martin Luther King's resistance strategies that had gone on for years, had finally hit the headlines. The most shocking event – one that changed the nation – was when black children marched for desegregation in Birmingham. Millions of Americans, via television, watched in horror as police used fire hoses that knocked the children down and tore off their clothes. Some were sloshed down sidewalks and over parked cars by the powerful jet streams. American children were being harmed by their supposed protectors. For a finale, the police let loose their attack dogs, further terrifying the children and shocking the nation's conscience.

President Kennedy spoke for the majority when he said the scenes made him sick to his stomach. He immediately initiated legislation that even after his assassination, became law. Every public facility in America, including schools, restaurants, hotels and swimming pools, had to be made available to all races. Silvia knew laws didn't mean much until they were implemented. But the 1964 Civil Rights Act provided hope and ammunition for Silvia and her fellow warriors to accelerate the legal war.

It was six o'clock – dinner time – that fateful night. Silvia stood over the stove, raw burger in one hand, ready to heat up the fry pan with the other. The kids had been fed early and were happily sprawled on the living room couch, eyes glued to Woody Woodpecker cartoons.

Suddenly, a voice blasted over the TV: "We interrupt this program to bring you a special news report."

Ignoring the muck on her hands, Silvia raced to hear the news. The announcer spoke in slow, staccato words: "Martin Luther King has been shot dead."

"Oh God!" Her hand flew to her chest. Alarm. Fear. Grief. Dazed, she flopped down beside her daughter. The boys, annoyed by the interruption, clamored for their cartoons to come back. Linda touched her mother's cheek.

"Mommy, what's the matter?"

She pulled herself out of shock and chose her words carefully to avoid upset. "A very great man has been hurt – but don't worry." She was glad the cartoons resumed before Linda could ask more questions. "I'll be upstairs."

Perched on the end of the bed, Silvia turned on the radio. Dr. King had stood with friends on a motel balcony when a sniper's bullet shot him in the face with such force he flew backwards onto the concrete. A white man was detected running away from the scene. His friends had rushed their beloved leader to a nearby hospital where he was pronounced dead.

Heat gripped her throat, her stomach churned. Gone was the great saint who led the way without violence – God, there'll be hell to pay for this. She laid down and curled into a tight ball but her apron twisted around her hip and she remembered the uncooked burgers left on the counter. As she struggled upright to get back to work, relief came.

"Daddy's home!" the kids shouted.

"Where's Mommy?" Frank asked.

"Up." Linda pointed. "She's sad."

In a flash he was in the bedroom. "I heard the news driving home." He pulled her into his arms and studied her face. "Are you okay?"

"Numb – needed quiet. But dinner . . . it's not finished." He brushed his fingers gently through her curls. His warmth soothed some of her tension but the thought of food made her gag.

"Forget dinner. I'll take the kids out for ice-cream and grab a bite there." Although Frank didn't feel compelled to fight for racial justice, he was especially kind in times of tragedy.

With the house clear, she turned on the TV. Riots were already underway in D.C. Bands of black teenagers paraded into Peoples Drug store and came out laden with bags of whatever they yanked off the shelves. Down the street, black men threw bricks into a liquor store window and cleared the shelves, right before the eyes of the viewing public. Her heart beat faster; perspiration wetted her arm pits.

Then the news got even worse. The TV networks went nation-wide and showed similar black mobs assembled in the streets of Baltimore, New York, Chicago and nearly every city in America. Shivers shot up her spine. After this live show of ruthless destruction and violent looting by blacks, what would happen to the newly gained public sympathy for integration?

For an entire week, when the kids were in school, a horrified Silvia watched as the riots continued, fully covered by radio, TV, newspapers and magazines. Defiant black men, women and children looted stores, smashed cars and burned down buildings, ironically in their own ghetto neighborhoods. It was a war zone. Smoke from fires filled the skies as tanks rolled down streets manned by gun-toting soldiers. Police, their faces masked in protective gear, let loose tear gas on hordes of rioters, who coughed and grabbed their faces, frantic to reach breathable air.

The reaction to the murder of Dr. King was not only spontaneous. It was savage and in-your-face bold. The facts could not be denied. Black Americans would no longer contain their deep frustration and rage.

Initially Silvia's dread merged with that of the masses. Then, from somewhere unknown, a sliver of hope crept into her attention. The riots were causing fear that the violence would spread into suburban neighborhoods. That fear could goad racism fighters – like herself – into a state of emergency. A state she knew most black Americans had been in for a very long time.

Within a week, her wish came true. An emergency meeting was called for the board members of the Unitarian churches that ringed Washington, D.C.

When she arrived at the nearly full conference room, Silvia nodded hello but maintained silence; the usual friendly chit-chat didn't feel right. The atmosphere was charged with restlessness. Something important was about to happen.

Harry Pine, the chairman, stood waiting to begin. In his mid-fifties, temples laced with gray brought out the blue in his eyes and dimples showed when he flashed one of his frequent smiles. His job as a project manager for the Central Intelligence Agency, and his friendly demeanor, won him the coordinator role for this group of white civil servants and housewives. He began with his usual straight talk.

"None of us came to agonize over the slaying of Dr. King or the riots. Instead, we've come to forge an action response to the tragic evil caused by racism. A team of us have put together a project we hope the rest of you will endorse. For this project to succeed our commitment in volunteer time is essential. Even more important is for each of us liberal white folks to find and purge our own condescending attitudes; like the belief that we know what's best for others."

Blood rushed to Silvia's face. His remarks were about last year's seminar when she had been shocked and embarrassed by the truth about why white people tended to be judgmental. The problem had come over with the Puritans. They had a mistaken religious belief that all people were born evil: sin is within. Since nobody wanted to see their own evil, fear of introspection became the societal norm. Even in modern times, that norm stayed intact. It was selfish to introspect. No navel contemplation allowed.

For Silvia, it was a eureka discovery. As a mother she knew children were not born evil. How could she have been so brain-washed into adopting such an ugly notion? There was no way to fix her own mistakes if she didn't look at them.

Equipped with the freedom to self-correct, she began to pay attention to her own conduct and often caught herself doing things she didn't like. One of the worst was when she dumped anger on the children when they (surprisingly) didn't do anything wrong. Instead the anger had spilled over from an unresolved argument with her sister.

Although her pride took a beating, it was outweighed by the virtue she felt when the change in herself was for the better.

Harry's team proposed to hire a black person to determine what needed to be done to solve problems brought about by racism. The project would be defined and implemented solely under black leadership. Black direction only. The Unitarians would supply the money and volunteer workers.

Excitement flooded Silvia. This project felt divinely inspired. She was eager to get involved.

When she got home, Frank was asleep. His six foot athletic body was sprawled across most of the bed; his rumpled brown hair made his handsome features look boyish. She wanted to kiss him awake and share the exciting news. But experience had taught he wasn't interested in her fight for justice, especially when he had to get up early for work.

She rolled onto her back and stared at the ceiling. Frank's disinterest bothered her. Yet why should she be bothered? He was racist himself when they first met. He used the N word frequently and made snide remarks until he finally quit to escape Silvia's tongue lashings about the irrationality of his bigotry. It wasn't that she could not love a racist; they simply had crossed wires in their thinking that needed to be untangled.

Sure enough, Frank's attitude changed, partly in response to Silvia's logic but mostly due to black players who joined his college football team. They became some of his best friends. So why didn't he applaud her efforts to rid others of those same racist attitudes? Like every human, Frank had to have been born with a desire to make the world a better place.

Something must have happened when he was a boy to shut him down.

To drill deeper for an answer would require pacing. She eased out of bed, slipped into her robe and tiptoed downstairs. With lit cigarette, she paced around the rooms – not a large space in their small Cape Cod. The beige wool carpet looked worn. Or was that just dirt? Tomorrow she would clean a bit; wipe the fingerprints off the wall by the telephone.

She exhaled and snuffed out the butt. So what caused Frank's indifference to saving the world? His father was a kind, soft-spoken man who was mostly cheerful. But she'd seen his fear of the unknown. One incident was particularly creepy.

She and Frank were on their way to his new job in Idaho. They said their good-byes and were headed to the car, when Frank's father shouted, "Wait!" He grabbed Frank by the arm. With tears in his eyes, he begged his son not to go. "What if it's not a nice place? What if the people are no good?" It wasn't just a case of being too attached to his son. He was genuinely afraid of what might be out there.

Frank wasn't going into outer space; he was going to Idaho. Silvia would have joked about the incident when they were underway, except for the shattered look on Frank's face. He wouldn't speak for the first hour of the drive and made it clear he didn't want to talk about his father's excessive fears.

His mother was kindhearted, but often tortured herself and everyone around her with worry. Her stress reached shrill levels when Frank went out of town with his football team. She fretted the whole time he was gone, afraid their bus might crash or Frank would get hurt in the game. Once on a cold day, Silvia stayed inside with her mother-in-law to keep warm while they watched Frank fix a flat tire. "What if the car falls off the jack? He'll be crushed!" Silvia was shocked at the intensity of fear over such a simple task.

She lit another cigarette and contemplated. How difficult it must have been for Frank as a child. To be constantly bombarded with worry would undermine anyone's self-confidence. No wonder Frank had no incentive to help build a better world; he didn't realize he could have any impact. And he probably worried that if he tried anything, he would be hurt in some way.

Her heart swelled with compassion for Frank – and for his parents – who no doubt got saddled with their fears from their own parents.

God, what harmful stuff was she laying on her own kids? She quickly snuffed her cigarette and hurried up to bed lest she lie all-night pondering *that* one.

2

In less than two months, ten black applicants for the job of director of the Unitarian project were thoroughly vetted by Harry Pine's team, CIA style. As secretary, Silvia took notes during the interviews and verified the financial information supplied by the applicants. Harry taught her to use code with bank officers to verify candidates' account balances. She had a hard time being serious when to verify $1,000, it was against the rules to say the exact amount. She had to ask if the balance was in the middle or low four figures. Obviously, bankers loved being covert and spy-like about money. They didn't think of money as a utility, like water and electricity.

Competition among the nine men and one woman who applied was intense. The job not only offered creative freedom with minimal oversight by a board of directors, it offered an annual wage of twice the medium income at $15,000 plus $10,000 for project expenses. Silvia scoffed at some of the recommendation letters that so exaggerated a candidate's qualities that even a deity could not have achieved such lofty heights.

But one candidate rose above the others, not for his scholarly credentials, political connections nor level of commitment to the cause. All the candidates were deeply committed and anxious to come up with strategies that would improve black lives. It was his ability to communicate well with a wide range of socio-economic types – from intellectuals to what he called street dudes – that won him the job. At age thirty-seven, John Darnell had worked as an auto shop owner, an air force sergeant and before age twenty-one, as a pimp.

As soon as notice came that he'd set up the office, Silvia telephoned.

"Hello. This is Unity House." His baritone voice sounded like he was smiling, not formal or distant. Silvia could be herself.

"What a great name!" Reflecting for a moment, she continued with passion, "really, really great." She paused, allowing space for John to respond. When he didn't, she continued. "Okay, I'm calling to volunteer to do whatever needs doing. I'm Silvia Nolan."

"Silvia who?"

"Nolan. We met at one of your many interviews. I'm with the team of Unitarians that wanted this project to happen."

"Oh yes, I remember you. You're the first to volunteer. Come on down. How about tomorrow at ten o'clock?" Short and sweet.

"I'll be there." She put her hand on her heart to calm the pounding. *This is it!* In the past, her work to end racism required persistence and patience since laws had to be changed. Unity House felt urgent; dynamic.

Her enthusiasm soared; then plunged. How would she get there? The office was in the city. The bus took too long. She would have to drive Frank to work to have a car and leave Unity House at two o'clock to be home by three when the kids got home. By four o'clock, they would all have to pile into the station wagon to fetch Frank home. But no matter all the driving; the cause was so important.

Then worry churned her stomach when she telephoned Frank at work to ask for his agreement with the plan. When he said yes, she gave thanks to God. It wasn't as if she had a plan B. Like many young families, Frank's salary barely covered living expenses. The options of hiring a regular babysitter or buying a second car could not be put on the table.

When she arrived at Unity House, Silvia was astonished to find a neighborhood undergoing classic gentrification. Small, dilapidated homes sandwiched between elegantly renovated townhouses seemed ironic since they were directly in sight of the U.S. Capitol where the fight for equal opportunity for all was supposed to take place. No doubt the run down homes were rentals occupied by poor people, mostly blacks, who soon would be driven out by skyrocketing market values.

Unity House was in a one-story brick townhome; its white paint fashionably antiqued. A gold designer porch lamp was mounted beside a freshly painted red door with gold latch and knocker. A recently trimmed boxwood hedge marked a tiny plot of well-kept grass on either side of the entrance walk.

Inside, a large plate glass window had been cut into the front room, providing extra light to the two small desks, large work table and file cabinet. A small oval cherry-wood table was centered under the window. It held a full pot of fresh coffee, filling the sunny space with an inviting aroma.

John was warm, cheerful and handsome, with wavy black hair and a slender yet muscular physique. His brown eyes twinkled within a face free of tension lines. He led Silvia on a tour through the house, which included his office – a room barely large enough for the used mahogany desk, armchairs and bookcase. The conference room was large, with a wooden table and folding chairs. A fresh coat of white paint and new carpeting throughout combined with the spartan furnishings to give a spacious aura to the small but charming work space.

John pulled two chairs up to the oval table. They sipped coffee and chatted about their personal lives. He'd been divorced for several years and had one teenage daughter who lived with her mother. His own apartment was within walking distance of the office. Their easy conversation revealed a mutual optimism for what Unity House might be able to do, and they shared a sense of urgency to get on with the work.

John told her they already had one client. "I was floored when the heads of the company came to me and said they wanted to know what it is like to be black. They actually used those words! So I asked them why, and they said they needed to understand all income levels of black people to design their stores as centers for community development. They said they'd provide jobs, training and in some cases even ownership." As he told the story, his eyes sparkled. He took a sip of coffee and chuckled. "Guess who it is?"

Silvia was dumbfounded. "Sounds enlightened. Don't know any such companies."

He leaned forward and slapped the table, "It's McDonald's! You know, the one with the golden arches."

"My God." Silvia smiled and clapped her hands. She already liked McDonald's for their low prices and family friendly atmosphere. It was the only restaurant she could afford to go for lunch with the kids. But if they truly were a community-development minded corporation, well, her like could grow into love. "So, how can you do it, get them inside black culture?"

"That's where I need your help. You can type, right? First we need a bibliography to help them do their homework. Books by black authors: Malcolm X, Stokely Carmichael, James Baldwin. I've made a list of about fifty." He handed her a few sheets of paper. "You've no doubt read most of them."

She had, but a big one was missing.

"What about *An American Dilemma?*"

"That's like a phone book." He shook his head, "I'm not gonna bury them in mental stuff. Besides, it's written by a white man."

For a moment, embarrassment shrouded Silvia for attempting to show how smart she was. John went to his office and came back with a pack of cigarettes. He lit one and handed her the pack, gesturing for her to take one. Relieved, she lit up.

John sat back down and exhaled, "So, here's the rest of my plan. After they do their reading, I'll lead them on a tour. Let them see street life. Some cons, some prostitutes, some drug stuff. They'll see the burned-out areas from the riots. I'll walk them inside the various housing situations – slums and mansions. I'll introduce them to a group of my friends, street dudes and educated types. Maybe we'll have a series of – what do you call them? – huddle sessions. They can get some one-on-one time with each other. And that's it." John studied her face, looking for her reaction.

"Sounds perfect. I especially like that you'll put them in the middle of the street life. Though it's hard for me to believe – an American corporation wanting to get down with poor black folks. Are they this hip or is there some catch? Do you believe them?"

John frowned; his lips tightened, "Let's say I believe their motives as much as I believe yours. We'll see how deep you white folks' commitment goes; how strong it is when the going gets rough." He looked her in the eyes, "We'll see about all of you all."

Silvia's face grew hot. She turned away from John's eyes. "Sorry to be so, so — um, what's the word? – arrogant." She took a drag on her cigarette.

He snuffed out his smoke and gave her a wide smile, "Am sure you'd like to get to work."

Thankful he cleared the air, she followed him to the desk that had a typewriter. Without a word, he handed her stencils and took the plastic cover off the mimeograph machine.

"You're all set, unless you need me to show you how to ink the machine?"

"Nope, I've got this." She had plenty of office experience while working her way through college. "Have you got correction fluid? I type fast, but to be honest, I make mistakes."

John raised his eyebrows, feigning surprise, and handed her a small bottle.

"What?" She grinned. "You didn't think I made mistakes?"

"Didn't think you'd admit to it."

When she finished, she could hear John on the phone so helped herself to another cup of coffee until he was available to proofread. The front door opened and in walked a man in a snazzy white Panama hat. His tall, slim figure was clad in a navy-blue suit with a white open-collared shirt. On his smooth bronze face, his ear-to-ear smile prompted Silvia to greet him like an old friend. "Love the fedora," she said and beckoned him to sit on the chair beside her.

"I'm Silvia, a volunteer. It's my first day."

"Well, hello, Silvia." He took off his hat. "I'm Elwood, a friend of John's."

He studied her with unusually deep, yet friendly eyes.

John came out of his office. "Hey, Elwood." They nodded to each other. Silvia sensed a flow of energy coming from them that startled her. She'd never noticed sensations like that before.

John pulled over another chair and sat down. Silvia handed him the stencils.

"What's happening?" Elwood asked.

"I've been working on the McDonald's thing, lining up contacts to meet with them. Everyone's willing so far. Silvia here's helping."

Elwood nodded his approval, "So, Silvia, tell me about yourself."

She laughed, "I feel like you already know all about me – "

John interrupted. "Silvia, I should tell you that Elwood here is my spiritual guru. If he seems strangely hip to you, just know he comes by it naturally."

She was surprised – didn't expect an ex-pimp to have a guru. But thrilled to make the acquaintance of a spiritual guide, she beamed at him. "I could feel something special about you." She tapped the side of her coffee mug. "What should I call you?"

"Elwood's fine. And you're right – I do know you and I'll tell you what you are." He put one hand softly on her arm. "You're a good person. A spiritual person. You've been sent here to do good things for the black movement. I'm glad you've come."

She scrunched down in her chair and felt heat flood her face. No one, not even her, had spoken out loud about her spiritual side before. Flustered, her hands moved nervously through her hair. It was a relief when John handed her the approved stencils so she could get back to work.

At the mimeograph machine she pondered Elwood's words. Did that mean she was expected to come up with enlightened – brilliant – ideas? An instant later, she knew the question was idiotic and snapped back into her normal clumsy self as she smudged the black ink all over her hands.

When her time at Unity House was over, Silvia struggled to tear herself away from what felt like God's work. She did beat the kids home and dutifully carried out the rest of the schedule.

With the children down for the night, Silvia and Frank watched an episode of *Gunsmoke*. With each commercial break, she chatted enthusiastically about her first day. Frank showed no interest, but she continued to share the details in hopes he would understand why she was needed at Unity House.

"I plan to go there two or three days a week. I'll drive you to work, get home in time for the kids, make dinner so when we get home with you, we can sit right down and eat. Will that work for you?" Her words were stilted, but she couldn't help how they sounded. She was anxious about his agreement and needed to make sure he got the facts.

"If you want to do all that driving, what can I say?" He turned his attention back to Marshall Dillon's exploits. Silvia silently cheered and beamed a big smile at the back of his head.

Four weeks later the McDonalds Corporation project was over and declared a huge success by everyone involved. John alone did the face-to-face work with the four senior managers – all white men in their early fifties – who went through his cultural emersion program. Silvia's job was to edit and type a report for the Unity House board from notes John voiced into a Dictaphone.

"Their faces were grim. It was like a pilgrimage when we schlepped through the charred remains of the buildings burned during the riots. The crunch of our feet through the broken glass was the only sound. We had to hold our noses to quash the horrific smell of moldy smoke. The devastation appeared to go far beyond from where we were standing. What upset them the most was the fact that it all happened in the poor neighborhoods. They remarked that a Marshall Plan was needed to restore what was equivalent to a war zone."

John was impressed by their sustained enthusiasm. "They didn't flinch when I took them to visit families at the East Capitol public housing…those dilapidated apartments where the stench of urine fills the hallways and graffiti covers the walls. I was touched by their eagerness to experience the cultural nuances first hand and pleased when they gave genuine respect to everyone."

Due to their lack of what John called typical arrogance, he helped McDonalds establish relationships with his contacts in other major cities. And because of the wisdom gained through John's program, the company created a community development department and hired a black director.

When she heard the facts, Silvia admitted to having been prejudiced against corporate America. Here was a company that acted on common sense. They knew if they gave goodwill to their employees and the communities around their stores, they would sell more burgers, shakes and fries.

The weeks passed by and Silvia's feelings for John took a turn toward the sensuous. He was in tune with her concerns about the world. They had the type of compatibility she longed for with Frank. Yet John didn't show any romantic feelings toward her, and she had no intention of doing anything about hers. After all, she was married.

At the same time, she could feel something…like an energy which radiated from him that was not about sex. When no one else was around, she asked him about it. He looked at her sideways, squinting his eyes as if she'd said something offensive. Then he laughed.

"Girl, you're not supposed to have that kind of awareness; just beguiled by my sterling personality without knowing why." He got up from his chair and paced around the desk. He was focused intensely on the floor, as if he could gather the words he wanted to say from the carpet. Then he sat back down and looked her in the eyes.

"Okay. You're the first that ever asked me about it. Elwood can explain it to you better."

She waited for him to continue. When he didn't, she asked how she could get some of that energy that so intrigued her.

"Ask Elwood."

One of Silvia's jobs at Unity House was to recruit and coordinate volunteers. Since the opening three months before, volunteers of all races, education and experience levels signed up. When Brad came in, offering to volunteer full time,

Silvia knew they had struck gold. In his late thirties, his hazel eyes sparkled when he said he was eager to get involved because a black led project could do things that mattered. Although he had a wife and two young children to support, he said his Jewish grandparents left him plenty of money and a mandate to do something to make the world a better place.

All volunteers professed an intense desire to get rid of the ravages of racism. John asked for and was presented with dozens of ideas for projects. All were scrutinized but none gained momentum, until finally, a star was born.

The first time the idea was mentioned was a day when Silvia was at Unity House. John burst in the front door and spoke without taking a breath.

"The new guy, Brad – the rich one you recruited – I checked him out. He's good. He's coming in tomorrow to start looking for ways we can deal with television's exclusion of blacks."

"Huh?" Silvia was blank.

"Have you heard of Nicholas Johnson?" John asked.

"Nope." Silvia drooped in her chair.

"He's a Commissioner on the FCC."

"What's FCC?"

"Okay. I didn't know what it was either when I first got wind of this. The Federal Communications Commission. They regulate the TV industry."

"So what about this Johnson guy? Is he black?"

"No. God girl, what world do you live in? Hell no! Nick Johnson isn't black. Nobody black is allowed into that world. But get this. Johnson blames the TV industry for the riots. He's on talk shows, news interviews – all over the place – saying they had a *legal* responsibility to let the public know the levels of frustration in black communities. And they failed. They broke the law." John's face gleamed with excitement. "Neat, huh?"

Silvia sprung out of her chair, "Fantastic! Everyone can see there are almost no black people on TV. All the broadcasters broke the law. Can we sue them?

"That's what we've got to figure out. The airways are public. Johnson shouted that out everywhere. *We* own them. Who knew? The broadcasters don't own anything. They have to be awarded a license. To win it they have to prove their programs serve the needs and interests of *everybody* in the cities they serve."

A surge of joy flooded Silvia. They were on to something. Something big. "The D.C. population is already seventy-five percent black." She shook her fists into the air.

"Damn straight. Black folks have not been served; not even close." John thrust his arms up in a victory stance. He spun around and faced Silvia, "You realize that *all* the big cities are majority black?"

Adrenaline rushed through her. "And, God, if we can sue them and get more blacks on TV… wow! That's the way to get black folks into white people's living rooms." This was the breakthrough they needed.

John bounced from one end of the room to the other, arms and hands in motion. Silvia purred, simultaneously excited and content. She saw the future. TV shows that featured the way of life of black folks could open the minds of people who only knew them in servile positions. Myths could be debunked. Prejudices dissolved like Frank's when he got to know his black team mates.

The phone rang and interrupted their euphoria. "It's for you." John handed Silvia the receiver.

"Yes, this is she. What?" It was the school. Frankie fell and maybe broke his arm. "I'll be there in half an hour. In the meantime, are you putting ice on it? Good. Good." She grabbed her purse, told John what had happened and ran out the door, nearly bumping into Elwood on his way in. "Sorry I've got to go. But I need to talk to you."

"I know," Elwood said. "Next time you come, I'll be here."

Worried about Frankie, Silvia pushed beyond the speed limit on the drive to the elementary school. He was a brave kid in most ways, not afraid of the dark or scary stories. When his sibs showed fear, he would ease them with his nine-year-old reasoning power. But his tolerance for pain was near zero. At the sight of a drop of blood anywhere on his body, he howled as if the end was in sight. The pain from a broken arm might devastate him.

When she reached the nurse's office, she breathed a relieved sigh. There he sat, happy and a bit heroic looking with his left arm in a sling. She sat on the cot beside him, cuddled him gently and kissed his cheek. "My brave boy. I thought I would find you in tears."

Frankie grinned and whispered in his mother's ear so the nurse couldn't hear. "It wasn't bleeding."

The diagnosis was a sprained wrist caused when he broke a fall from the jungle gym. If he kept it in the sling and iced it after school, he would be good to go in three or four days. To Frankie's disappointment and his mother's delight, the injury wasn't sufficient to keep him out of school. He only got excused from recess.

Like most mothers, Silvia held her children in high esteem from the moment they were born. She enjoyed being immersed in their innocence and cheered them on through each development stage. Not that jealousy, possessiveness, and fierce competition didn't arise. To her, sibling warfare and tantrums were opportunities to hone their character and improve her motherly skills. Before Unity House, she felt confident that her quality time with her children was kept in balance with time spent fulfilling her need to rid the world of racism. But tension in the household grew as her Unity House work increased and time with the family declined.

On one of her days at home, five-year-old Alan bounded in from the backyard with a caterpillar balled up for protection in his carefully cupped hands. Silvia was on the phone.

"Mom! Mom! Look! Feel it."

Alan put the fuzzy brown ball close until it touched her nose. In the past, she would have matched his excitement with her own. This day she was at a crucial point in her conversation with a potential volunteer lawyer who wanted details about the TV project. Rather than push Alan away and break his heart, she pulled him close and put him on her lap without a break in her phone conversation. But Alan wasn't fooled. He knew her attention wasn't on him or his treasure. He angrily pushed her face away from the phone until the receiver fell to the floor.

"No! No! No!" he shouted and sobbed as he ran out into the backyard. She knew she should end the call and go make amends with her little boy. Instead, she decided Alan could wait and maybe the volunteer would not, so she picked up the phone and resumed her recruitment push. Alan's psyche was put on the back burner.

Silvia finished the conversation but stayed at the desk, head down on folded arms. Her heart ached over what just happened with Alan. There was no doubt about the work at Unity House. It was essential; a unique opportunity to make progress in the fulfilment of her lifelong mission. But she couldn't push the kids away. Somehow, she would have to convince the children that her lack of attention on them didn't mean she loved them less.

She lifted her head when Linda came trudging in.

"Mom why are you always on the phone?"

Yes, Silvia needed to do something to bring her passions – loving her kids and ending racism – together. This wasn't the first time Linda had whined about Silvia's distraction. When she heard Linda's question, almost an accusation, she knew Alan had complained to his sister. What to say? She patted her lap urging Linda to sit. They hugged. Then without any idea of what to say, she faced her daughter and spoke spontaneously.

"I'm trying to help things get better for people who aren't as happy as us. It's a time when changes can happen, and I need to do my part. Just because I'm busy doesn't mean I don't love you guys. It's for the love of you and all children in the world that I must try to make things better. Don't you want me to do that?"

Grateful Linda had asked the question, she continued. "Do you remember when you asked me what a nigger was?"

Linda nodded.

"And do you remember what I said?"

"You said it was a bad word for a black person."

"And didn't I say we needed to help people who used that word feel better about black people so they wouldn't call them bad names?"

"Uh huh. So is that what you're doing?"

"That's what a bunch of people are trying to do at Unity House. Would you like to come downtown and see?"

"Yes!" Linda brightened. "When can I come?"

"When school's over for the summer, I'll take you."

Satisfied, Linda skipped outside to play with her brothers.

Elwood was already at Unity House when Silvia arrived on her regular day. He and John sat with coffee in the front room.

"Is this a private meeting?"

John pulled up another chair.

"We need a lawyer to tell us how we can go after the TV networks. I was just about to call around and find somebody."

Elwood closed his eyes and appeared to go into meditation. Several minutes later he said, "Go ahead and make your calls. You'll get some good lawyers."

John went into his office. Elwood turned to Silvia. "So you want to know how you can get the strong vibrations you feel from me and John?"

She wondered how he knew. John must have told him.

"You wouldn't have noticed it unless you had a few strands of this energy awakened inside yourself. Go find some books about self-realization and see where they lead you."

"Is that it?"

"You expected a long lecture? I don't do lectures. I'm the strong, silent type." He winked at her, and she immediately thought of her complaints about Frank being the same type. She had never discussed Frank with Elwood.

They sat together in silence for some time. She relaxed and felt good; everything in harmony. Whatever this power was, it was extraordinarily soothing. She began to fathom Elwood's powerful method of helping people be at their best.

The following Tuesday, a day she wasn't scheduled for Unity house and the kids had gone to school, the phone rang.

"Hi, John. Um, no, it's not my day. What's up?"

"It suddenly worked out to be a good day for a slew of volunteers to come here to talk about the TV thing. Can you be here?"

"Let me see if I can find someone to take the kids. I'll call you back." God, the legal war was about to be mapped out. She couldn't miss it.

Sally, a neighbor whose three kids were best friends with Silvia's, agreed to intercept them after school. Silvia called for a ride and hurried into fresh clothes.

As the taxi drove her across town, Silvia's stomach hurt. The expense would probably trigger Frank to punish her with his painfully effective silent treatment that could last for days.

Her troubles did not subside until she reached Unity House and saw the group of fellow warriors assembled. John patted the chair beside him.

"And this is Silvia, our volunteer coordinator. The rest of you go ahead and introduce yourselves."

Silvia was glad to see Harry Pine since his presence gave a high level of stability to the team. A slim black woman Silvia didn't know introduced herself as Jackie Tyler, assistant director of communications for a nation-wide religious organization. She looked to be in her mid-forties and wore a well-tailored olive-green suit with a rose-colored blouse and high heels. Her polished look made Silvia feel underdressed in her plaid skirt, red sweater and black flats. But never mind. Her attention snapped back into place and she cheered silently when Jackie mentioned her church had experience with a legal battle against a TV station for black exclusion.

Silvia was also elated to find two communication lawyers in the room. One was George Hardy, white and handsome with a crew-cut, who operated his own not-for-profit law firm. His casual dress of jeans and navy blazer made him look younger than she'd pictured when they'd talked on the phone. The other lawyer was new to her. He introduced himself as Barry Wells, president of a black lawyers organization. He too was handsome, with dimples and deep brown eyes. She guessed he was with a corporate law firm since he was dressed formally in suit and tie.

"Jackie," John said, "tell us about your TV license challenge experience."

"It was a landmark case. Happened in Jackson, Mississippi. The first time the court gave legitimate standing to a group of black and white citizens. We filed a petition that challenged the renewal of a TV station's license." She spoke slowly, with enthusiasm, like a teacher who knew how to keep the attention of her class.

"Before our case, the consumers of television – that's us, the public, mind you – weren't allowed to be heard in court for or against the renewal of a TV station's license. Imagine that, in America where we the people own the airwaves? But thanks to a young black law student who led the charge, we did win the right to be in court and to file a legal case against renewing a TV station's license because they didn't provide programs relevant to the needs and interests of sixty percent of their viewing population – who happen to be black.

"What does the citizens' group get if the TV station's license isn't renewed?" Harry asked, "do they get the license?"

George raised his hand. "I'll answer that," he said. "It's a whole other ball game to own a license to broadcast. It costs millions in start-up capital and requires a business plan showing expertise in the technical aspects of broadcasting. We're not going after the license for ourselves. We'll put together what's called a petition-to-deny license renewal."

Barry, animated and smiling from the start of the meeting, finally got a turn to speak. He lept out of his chair. "This strategy is tremendous! George and I talked about it on the way here. It's the first I heard of it, but wow!" His hands gestured dramatically. "Does everyone here realize that not just D.C. but every major city in America has a majority black population? Without doubt this is a slam dunk!"

The group erupted with excited chatter. John, his smile ear to ear, held up a hand for quiet. "Okay, okay, we agree that this is a humongous opportunity to bring about real change." His expression turned serious as he met the eyes of the others. "But can we do it? How do we put together this petition and against who?"

Jackie pulled papers out of her briefcase. "This is a guide we put together for how to do it. And the FCC has published material about what they require."

"I have some timely news," George said. His face was stoic, but his eyes glistened. "We just won a grant that will fund us for several years. This means our firm can give free services to community projects just like this one." A big grin broke his composure.

Everyone gave kudos, but for Brad, that wasn't enough. He jumped out of his chair. "My God, you mean you'll be able to work on this full time?" When George nodded, Brad lifted his arms toward the ceiling. "This feels like more than a coincidence."

Chills went up Silvia's spine.

Jackie brought everyone back to earth when she said it would take about three months to put together the petition. "One thing we'll need is a team to watch all the D.C. stations, from the beginning of their broadcast day until sign-off, seven days a week for several weeks. We have to document whether or not their programming is relevant to a black audience and how many black people are on the air." She tapped on the table. "And that's just the beginning. There are many more requirements needed to document black exclusion. This won't be easy."

As the taxi sped towards the suburbs past the rows of embassies on Massachusetts Avenue, Silvia noticed the lack of traffic. Usually it moved slow enough for her to read the country names on the door plaques. But, thank God, they were ahead of rush hour. Plenty of time to get back before the kids. She rested her head on the back of the seat and basked in the joy bubbling inside her, undaunted by the foul odor from the so-called air freshener the driver had installed.

Uplifted by the TV strategy, she mused about the future. For one thing, with black news producers at the helm, human rights events would be breaking news. From a woman's perspective, that would be a good thing. And dramas – sitcoms like *I Love Lucy* – would laugh with black folks about their lives. The beauty of the black culture would be revealed on television. And viewers that didn't already know would find out that beyond the skin, humans are all pretty much the same.

She chuckled out loud at her day-dreams; then checked the rear-view mirror. The driver wasn't looking at her like she was crazy. They drove past the National Cathedral with its elegant steeples, bell towers and perpetual scaffolding indicating it was still unfinished. Silvia remembered how the church's austerity humbled her and her high school friends who behaved like saints when their acapella choir sang there for Christmas services. Normally, at school during choir class, they behaved like hooligans.

When the cab crossed into Maryland, worry took over. She'd be home in fifteen minutes. Her body stiffened. What if Frank found out about her expensive ride? She bit her thumbnail. It felt awful to hide her activities from him. Why couldn't he just be excited for her stepping fully into her life's dream? No, her life's purpose. The world was changing and she was a part of that change. Couldn't Frank rejoice with her?

At the same moment the taxi dropped her off, the kids arrived from Sally's. Cabs were a rare phenomenon in the suburbs. Frankie and Alan, who were already car fanatics, were curious about the strange vehicle. What kind of car was it? Why was she in it? Why did it have a number with a funny light on top?

That evening, as soon as Frank walked in the door, the kids immediately shared the highlight of their day.

"Mommy rode in a taxi cab!"

Frank looked quizzically at Silvia. "What's that about?"

"Emergency meeting at Unity House. You won't believe the legal strategy that's landed in our laps." She nearly shouted in hopes her enthusiasm would be contagious.

"I'm not sure our budget can afford that kind of emergency. How much?"

She cringed. "Fifty dollars, tip included. I know. It's an outrageous amount, but we've found a legal way to force television to put more blacks on programs, newscasts and everything. Frank, just imagine – "

He put up his hand to stop her and turned his attention to the kids.

Two days later, on their drive to Frank's office, he abruptly pulled over and stopped on the side of the road. Frank snarled out his words. "What are you doing?" His eyes were full of anger. She had never seen him so aggressive. Never. She kept her eyes on his but her body stiffened defensively.

"I'm doing what I tell you I'm doing." Her throat clamped tight, so her voice was hoarse.

"What's really behind all of this interest in Unity House? It feels like you're pulling away from our family."

Blood rushed to her head. Anger overwhelmed fear. "This work I do, it's always for the family. For all families. God, if I put on a military uniform and marched off to war, you'd be proud of me. Well, for God's sake, isn't it time we prevented a war? Stopped the violence? How can you send your kids out into a world with all this hate and not show them you're trying to make it better? What's your *problem*?" She felt herself go off any semblance of balance, but to hell with it.

"How does what you've got yourself into show them anything? You're either gone, or if you're home, you're on the phone." His anger matched hers.

"Don't you know they watch and listen? They don't miss a thing. You should know that – you were a kid once. Linda asked me the other day why I was on the phone so often, and I told her."

"What did you tell her? Mommy's out saving the world?"

Silvia calmed herself before she answered Frank's sarcasm. "Something like that, only more specific. I told her I was trying to help people who use the word nigger change their attitudes – that's what I told her."

Frank went silent. She could see he thought of something he didn't want to say.

"Say it," Silvia pleaded. "Just say it."

He stayed silent, drove to his office, got out of the car and slammed the door.

Her anger stayed strong as she drove downtown. It was true – her excitement about the Unity House project didn't end when she got home. How could it? Why should it? It was the first time in years and years of frustrating, tedious work that a strategy with such potential – such tremendous hope for real change – was before her. She knew she was essential; she had the organizational skills to make this thing happen. No, not only her, but her for sure. She wished Frank would want to understand why it was so important. She wished he would give her that respect.

John was waiting for her when she walked in the door. "Tonight there's a work session with the United Church people. I need you here."

Her determination still heightened, it bled into her voice. "I'll be here." Too loud, she quickly dialed back to normal volume. "Do you have any idea who can help us monitor all the area stations for two weeks without gaps?" She'd been worrying about how that piece would get done.

"Yeah." John smiled, and his eyes lit up. "There's a welfare rights organization that has a lot of beautiful black mothers who are happy to watch TV for a cause. They're the ones who did it for the Mississippi petition. Jackie's coming tonight to help us get started."

"Okay. That's a great group of ladies – a load off my mind." Her anger completely forgotten, Silvia leaned back in her chair, her hands folded on the back of her head. "It's like the gods are with us on this one. Everything falls neatly into place."

On the drive home with Frank, Silvia told him there was another critical meeting at Unity House that night. "I know you're fed up, but please try to understand."

"Yeah, I do understand. Maybe better than you."

He glanced her way. She could hear the rancor in his tone. Stress filled her stomach. Was he afraid she was helping some dangerous group? "What do you understand?" She was puzzled. Frank locked into his silent-treatment and would not explain.

That night, Jackie put Silvia's mind at ease with clear details about how to train and schedule the volunteers to monitor the TV stations. Afterwards, John invited Silvia over to his place. At first she was surprised; then assumed he had information to feed her spiritual hunger.

When they entered the dark apartment, he took her arm and guided her to the couch. He sat down also, very close. So close he touched her hip with his. He reached his arm around her to turn on a small lamp, and to her dismay, let it rest on her shoulder.

"Hey!" She pulled away. "What's going on?" His behavior seemed odd; almost wooden, like it was staged.

"Just testing." He laughed and pulled his arm away but stayed close. Looking her right in the eyes, he said, "I could swear you were putting out some sensuous vibes toward me. Was I wrong?"

Yikes. Could he read her private sensations? Her heart pounded. Heat filled her face. "Um . . . no, you weren't wrong. But I'm married and don't act on sensuous vibes." She nervously smoothed her hair. The thought that her feelings, no matter how restrained, might mess up their Unity House work crossed her mind. That would be a real calamity. Oh God, how to get this into a good place?

It was John who saved what he almost wrecked. He stood and beamed a smile at her; his hands relaxed on his hips. "This was a test, and you passed. Congratulations!" He took her by the hands and pulled her up. "Come on, I wanna show you something." Bewildered, she timidly followed him into the kitchen. He turned on the light and there, at the kitchen table, sat Elwood.

"Hey, girl. Hope you're not mad at us." Elwood gave her a pleading smile. "We just had to know if you were serious about the work or if John was the draw." Elwood patted the chair next to him. Silvia sat, trying to deal with a mixture of anxiety and embarrassment. On cue, she felt her face flush.

"Coffee?" John asked.

"Please." Her voice cracked. She swallowed to clear her throat. "Sorry. Your test, it was a shock. But no doubt I'd have done the same thing if I were you. I guess you can't quite trust a white person."

Both men smiled and looked down at their coffee.

She checked her watch, saw the late hour. "Sorry, I've got to get home; early call in the morning."

John walked her to the car. "All is well?"

"Nothing to worry about." She smiled and waved goodbye.

On the way home, she wondered what would have happened if she had responded in kind to John's embrace. End of her Unity House work? The whole episode gave her the creeps.

It was midnight when she got home and Frank, in his pajamas, greeted her at the door. He was furious. "Why so late?"

Her voice calm, she explained that the meeting was a long one. He had worked himself into a frenzy that caused him – thankfully – to abandon the silent treatment.

He blurted out, "Are you in an affair with John?"

Judas. So that was what bothered him. Thank God she hadn't succumbed to her fleeting desire.

"No, I'm not." She felt pride. "And I'm not interested in stupid stuff. I'm interested in ridding America's soul of racism. That's it." Tonight had confirmed that, luckily.

He looked taken aback. He believed her but was genuinely surprised. Then he shook his head, still angry. "You've kept me awake. This has got to stop." He put an end to further conversation when he stormed upstairs. She waited until she heard him snore before she followed.

Silvia lay rigidly beside her husband, eyes wide open. So John and Elwood weren't the only ones that perceived she had an interest in John; so did Frank. If only that unfaithful thought had never entered her mind; especially since, to her chagrin, it was so obvious. Yet it was time she faced the truth about her marriage. Her patience with Frank's lack of support for her mission had come to an end. She was fed up with his narrow minded, selfish attitude toward her Unity House work. It was bad enough that he attempted to make her feel like a neglectful wife and mother; but the children could sense the turmoil. The most important value she wanted her kids to have when they grew up was a loving sense of service to God, country and their fellow human beings. For such service to be fulfilled and sustained, they would need to be surrounded by family and friends that supported and cared for them. Frank's love and support ended when duty took her away from the family. It dawned upon her that this difference was unreconcilable. Silvia thrashed about all night with thoughts of *to hell with him* on the one hand and *forgive* him on the other.

The next day she fixed breakfast as usual. Frank was cheerful with the kids, but without a word to her – no good morning or goodbye – he went off to work. Damn him. His silent treatment . . . she was fed up. As soon as the kids left for school, she lit a cigarette and sat at her desk.

How could they carry on as husband and wife when they were so out of sync? That thought made her snuff out her cigarette since to inhale with so much agitation took away her breath. Yet despite the emotional trauma, she had to find a solution quickly because Frank was fed up with her Unity House work at the exact time she needed to be there full time.

Divorce. The dreaded thought forced its way into her brain like water that shattered a dike. She ran her hands through her hair and lit another cigarette.

The phone rang. It was Brad who needed to know when she could come to plot out all the steps required to put the petition together. The normal sound of her voice belied the inner turmoil. She told him she wasn't sure but would try for tomorrow.

Just as she was turning back to continue agonizing over the crisis, Frank called. "I'm coming home to talk. Please be there." His tone was curt.

God, what was he gonna say? He wanted to talk? *That's different*, she thought sarcastically. Then she shook her head and told herself to get out of that mode. She slipped into jeans and her pretty green blouse, tidied up the living room and made a fresh pot of coffee.

When he arrived, Frank marched to the armchair and sat down without a glance at her. He took the coffee she handed him and lit a cigarette. "I wanna talk about us." His voice was strained, and he continued to avoid eye contact although she sat directly across from him. Her legs trembled. They sipped coffee and smoked. Silence reigned for some moments.

"I can no longer live with your Unity House thing. It's always here when you're home, or you're always there when you're gone. You either quit it or quit us, me and the kids. It's not right what you're doing." While he spoke, he kept his eyes down, elbows on the arms of the chair; chin resting on his hands.

Her heart pounded louder. Frank had just delivered an ultimatum. Anger rose. She was determined not to argue with him so needed time to cool down. "Give me a minute?" He nodded.

She took a breath and then dropped the bomb.

"Frank, it's time to talk about divorce." She looked him in the eyes; he quickly looked away. "It's not that I don't love you. It's just not like a husband and wife anymore. We don't seem to . . . It's like I'm not helping you grow and you're not helping me. We're holding each other back."

Frank frowned and moved his head slowly back and forth. She read the movement as disgust. He stood and began pacing. "What the hell are you talking about? How can you say you love me at the same time you want a divorce?" He sat again, despair clouding his face.

Compassion for him welled up. She wished he would cry so she could cry with him.

"I've got to think about this by myself." He stomped upstairs.

A mixture of relief and sickening gloom crawled into Silvia's being. To break the vows – *until death do us part* – brings pain and suffering with no finality. Yet to remain in a marriage devoid of respect torments the souls of both.

At dinner that night, the air was thick with pain, yet the children didn't seem to notice.

"I won the spelling bee today!" Linda was thrilled.

"Really? What words did you spell?" Silvia tried to sound light.

"*Whistle* – " Linda began her list but her older brother interrupted with his usual taunts.

"Oh, that's so easy. Who couldn't spell that?" As a fifth-grader he was far superior to his third-grade sister.

Alan – as always – moved in as peacemaker. "I can't spell whistle. I can't even do it."

"Okay, guys, let's just eat and then you can go outside and play until dark," Frank said. When Dad spoke, everyone complied.

With the children outside, Silvia and Frank lingered at the table.

"What will happen with the kids?" Frank asked. "I'm telling you right now, there's no way I'm living anywhere without them." He was adamant.

Stunned, Silvia looked away. Tears welled. "I-I haven't thought about it."

"Don't think about you and the kids in one place and me in another, because that is not the way it's going to be. I'll take you to court."

Her voice trembled. "I . . . I will not fight with you about any of this, especially not the kids." She sobbed out the words. "We can't let them see us upset like this." Sacrifice the children? Her sobs exploded when the thought filled her with death-like grief. She rushed away where the children could not hear.

The next day, the home phone never stopped ringing. Word about the petition strategy spread rapidly. When people called Unity House to volunteer, they were given Silvia's number. One of the callers was Clarice, a woman she knew from church. When Silvia told her about a meeting the next night at Unity House, she asked if Clarice needed directions.

"No, I was there yesterday," Clarice said. "John and I talked for a long time. He's an amazing man. Do you know . . . this is embarrassing, but I'll ask anyway – is he married?"

Silvia tried not to react. "He's divorced."

"I can't wait to get started. Is there something I can do now – like today – any phone work?"

Was she after John or interested in the project?

"Let me see. I'll figure something out and call you back. Say, do you type? Okay, I'll be in touch." Silvia heard the edge in her own voice.

Clarice was Silvia's age, a beautiful divorcee with long auburn hair and a perfectly proportioned body. She had sufficient alimony so didn't have to earn an income. When they'd worked together on fair housing issues, Silvia found Clarice to be the type of volunteer not eager to dig in and do whatever needed doing. Instead, she required precise direction and was picky about what she would and wouldn't do. And she was certainly open about her romantic interest in John.

Even though Silvia felt threatened by her for some dark reason, Clarice's enthusiasm to volunteer, whatever the motive, needed to be nurtured. Silvia called Brad.

"I have a woman who doesn't have to hold a job for a living and wants something to do. She's from my church and about our age. I think she could do research if it had a narrow focus and you could guide her a little. You have anything? I'm sure she'd be willing to go to any library; she has a car."

Brad agreed to call Clarice and find out what she was capable of and set something up.

To keep her attention off the family crisis, between phone calls Silvia read the books she'd found about self-realization. The messages were varied – some psychological, some spiritual. Those that spoke in plain English described self-realization as the final step in evolution as mortals transcend from mere humans into spiritual beings, filled with much more physical love. The knowledge is ancient; first written about over twenty thousand years ago in Sanskrit language. Today's religions all refer to the energy by different names: the *Holy Spirit* in Christianity, the Hebrews named it *Shekinah*, the Muslims the *Ruh*, and the Hindus the *Kundalini*.

Despite a thorough search, she was disappointed. None gave practical information about how to get there. And today's reading alarmed her with the revelation that Buddha spent twenty-five years of grueling self-discovery before he got his realization. No way did she want to wait that long. Her frustration lingered until the phone rang, and brought her back to the present.

It was Frank. The anguish in his voice was greater than she'd ever heard from him, except when his father died. "I've got some questions that need answering."

"Right now?"

"Yes, now!" His voice was grating. "Why is it you really want this divorce? I don't understand, so tell me again."

When Silvia first became troubled about her marriage, she couldn't imagine not loving Frank. Where would the love go? The issue was critical to her confusion about divorce so she sought answers at the library. It was *The Art of Loving* that gave her clarity from the explanations of the various types and levels of love.

"Frank, it's not because I don't love you. I'll always love you. You're the nicest, kindest man . . . A great father. We're just not on the same wavelength and this is causing us not to grow; not to reach our potential. Neither one of us is getting what we need from the other to get to a higher place. That's the reason."

There was a long silence. "That's a lot of bull. This crap doesn't make any sense." The phone went abruptly dead.

Before she could process their conversation, the kids bounded in from school. They were happy to be home, eager to greet their mother and ready for free play. She was grateful to bathe in their exuberance and postpone her anguish.

After the kids had gone to bed, Frank and Silvia again tried to talk about the divorce. They lit cigarettes and sipped beer. "We have to get a lawyer," Frank said.

"And it should be one that will let us work out the details ourselves. I will not fight about anything in court."

A few years before, Silvia had witnessed a girlfriend's court case. The friend had been divorced for years and had custody of their three children, when she began a serious relationship with a black man. Her ex-husband immediately went to court for custody of his children, with the claim that his wife committed a crime.

Sure enough, the state of Maryland still had laws on the books that forbade the races to marry or have sexual relations. The elderly white judge, who was a member of one of Maryland's oldest wealthy tobacco farm families, didn't even bother to listen to the wife's side of the story. Within minutes of the deliberations, he ruled in favor of the husband and took away her friend's children. Silvia's grief for her friend – and her outrage over the fact that such laws were active in the United States of America – lingered.

Frank rubbed his brow. His face was contorted and colorless; he could barely speak. He said he didn't want to fight in court either.

Silvia had researched the grounds for divorce. "For twelve months we have to live separate places without interruption and no sex. But then, if we go ahead with the divorce, it's automatic. There's nothing more to it."

"That's all we need to do? Live in separate places for a year and then it becomes a legal divorce?" Frank lightened up. But for Silvia, the possible loss of every day with her kids cut so deep into her heart, misery flooded her brain. Until some of the pain subsided, further negotiations would have to wait.

3

The next morning's drive downtown soothed Silvia's tortured soul and filled it with splendor. Nature's bounty was at its height. The cherry blossoms had finished their reign and handed over the glory to delicate white and pink dogwood petals and scarlet hues of azaleas. Silvia's depression faded into grateful thanks to the city planners who kept the physical beauty of the nation's capital as a tribute to Mother Nature. No doubt they hoped the noble aesthetics would uplift the hearts and minds of ordinary citizens and if they were lucky, even an occasional politician.

At Unity House, everyone worked quietly until Silvia, who just ended a phone conversation, exclaimed loudly as she sped into John's office, "I think our lines are tapped – I always hear clicking. Do you hear it?"

John rolled his eyes. "Hey girl, this is Washington, D.C. The CIA, the NSA and the FBI – most especially the FBI because J. Edgar Hoover's scared to death of black folks – means there is no doubt. They *are* listening."

Silvia pondered for a moment. "Okay, maybe I'm naïve. But frankly, I hope they are. Let them hear us plan and plot all this legal action. That way they'll get comfortable. We're not doing anything to bring them – "

John interrupted. "That's fine for you white folks to think. I don't trust those guys. If they don't like what we do, they'll swoop in and call it illegal any time they want to. Thanks to God we have the CIA on our board and a good brother in the Department of Justice. I hope they've got us covered if we need them. But it's a fact of life for black people. We're always being scrutinized and hassled some kind of way. I'm not gonna worry about a little wiretap."

Brad strolled in from the conference room. "Not worry about what? I've just discovered something to worry about."

"Not to worry about the fact that our telephone lines are tapped. What's your worry?" John asked.

"Really? Our lines are tapped? Thought I was paranoid with all the click, click, click. So they listen to my wife remind me to pick up the bread and milk on the way home, and they use my tax dollars to do it." He shook his head and mumbled something about government bureaucracy, but then pointed to a thick report he'd brought with him. "My worry is that there are about three hundred people on one TV station's list of the so-called community leaders they said they'd interviewed. We know about five of them are black. After that we have to find out how many more are black, and I'm not sure how we're gonna do that."

Silvia knew exactly how. "That's easy. We have volunteers wanting to do phoning. We'll just call everyone on the list and ask them what color they are."

Brad and John looked at each other with raised brows. "Um . . . folks may react. It's a tricky question," John said.

"Don't worry. We'll figure out a discreet way. We can tell them we're a research firm working on race relations. That's a true statement."

"Okay. Go for it," Brad said. "I'll make a list for you. Or could someone take it to the law firm and make a copy?" Brad's tone changed to complaint mode. "John, we need our own copy machine. Stencils and mimeographing just don't cut it for times like this. We're trying to wage a legal war here with number two pencils."

"I know. I know. We've gotta take time out to put together a proposal. Maybe we'd better stop this petition work and do that first. We need a secretary, and you two should get some kind of pay. At least gas money back and forth, ya think?"

Silvia had written proposals for several civil rights projects so had knowledge of how to adapt to government and foundation requirements. "I could concentrate on the proposal and let Brad stay focused on the petition."

John shook his head. "Trouble is you aren't here enough. It takes someone working closely with me and you can't do this from home. What about Clarice? I'll see if she could give us a week or so to work it out."

Silvia's stomach clenched. Jealousy. Judas Priest, what a dumb reaction. But she had to admit to it. What if Clarice took over her place at Unity House?

A deathlike pall loomed over the Nolan household. Hence the children were more irritable than usual. Then too, Silvia's parents reacted with extreme upset when they got the news. Her mother, Helen, was apoplectic. She delivered several lectures over the phone, but today, after the kids left for school, she came in person to serve her diatribe.

Silvia understood her angst. She felt compassion for her mother whose constant companions of fear and worry blocked any desire to try to understand Silvia's reasons for the divorce. They sat on the couch facing each other.

"I just can't understand. You would break up your family because of some . . . I don't know what. Quest? You always were so damned bullheaded about what you thought was right." Her voice was tight and scratchy. "We knew you and Frank came from seriously different family beliefs, but now you have three wonderful children. How can you even consider divorce? The effect it will have on them will hurt them for a lifetime; ruin their chances for healthy relationships. Why?" Her face was red; tears welled in her eyes. "The children are the victims."

Helen's stress was infectious; it flooded Silvia's chest. She looked away. But her certainty didn't waiver. The children will be better off once the suppression caused by their mismatched parents was removed. Both she and Frank would open more fully when they stopped trying to fit into each other's agenda. They'd become happier people. With their parents free to be themselves, the children too would blossom.

Silvia had shared this intuition with her mother several times, but the result was an escalation of rage. This time, Silvia tried to avoid the usual reaction and offered what she suspected was a weak defense.

"You know we've tried to resolve our issues. We went to that disastrous couple's encounter session. And we've met with Reverend Cross every week. After all, he's a Harvard Divinity School graduate."

"Yes, but it seems he just gives you a platform to firm up your…your *whatever*. You come out of these sessions more certain." Helen's anger turned to grief. She put her head in her hands and sobbed quietly.

To comfort, Silvia put her arm around her mother's shoulders. She spoke softly. "I know you want to prevent this because you love us. But you'll see. When Frank and I separate, the kids will get clear and happy and be alert like never before. You'll see."

"Oh for God's sake." With a contemptuous jerk, Helen pulled out of her daughter's embrace, stormed out to her car, and yelled her final advice. "What you need is a good psychiatrist!"

Ouch. Her own mother thought her insane. The blow hit her heart, worse than a slap across the face. Yet once the hurt faded, her conviction held. With or without the support of her family, she would do what she had to do.

A week later, Silvia was reading at her desk, lit cigarette in hand, when Frankie burst through the front door.

"Hey, Mom, we're home!" Linda and Alan were close behind. Frankie pointed to her cigarette. "You have to stop that. It can kill you; causes cancer. Your smoke hurts us too."

"Wha – ?" She smashed the burning end into an ashtray. Cancer? Smoke hurts the kids? "Who told you this?" Her question came out defensively.

"We learned it at school. The teacher said to go home and tell our parents to quit cigarettes. We saw a movie about it."

Linda and Alan watched wide-eyed.

"Oh – kay." She took a deep breath. Right was right. She raised her hands in surrender. "I will stop. Soon."

"If you don't, I'll take your cigarettes and flush them down the toilet." Frankie kept the upper hand with his new authority.

"Whoa. Did your teacher tell you to do that too?"

"No. But I don't want you and Daddy to die."

Judas Priest, they've scared him. To quit now would be impossible with all the stress. Still, no more smoking when the children were around.

"Mom, can we have juice and cookies?" Alan changed the subject as he pulled at Silvia's arm and led everyone into the kitchen.

When Frank got home, Frankie continued to vent his new authority. "Daddy, you have to quit smoking cigarettes."

"Really? Who says?"

Frankie told him about the movie and what he learned.

"Well – um – uh." Frank's eyebrows shot up; he drew back his head. His recovery was quick and he put his arms around Frankie. "Son, thanks for the good advice. I hope this knowledge keeps you from smoking when you get older. What do you think?"

"I'm never smoking cigarettes," Frankie said. His sibs chimed in with *me neither.*

When the children were down for the night, Frank and Silvia immediately lit up to fulfill their long-delayed after-dinner smoke. They joked about how well the school equipped their son to revolt against his parents' bad habit and agreed the strategy was brilliant – instant checkmate. No longer, in good conscious, would they be able to smoke when their children were around.

Silvia felt euphoric. Like normal times, the couple laughed together. Maybe her wish would come true and they would part as good friends. Her optimism was quickly dashed when Frank jerked them back to their grim task.

"I talked to a lawyer, and just like you said, we can go the separation route and have an amicable divorce after a year. So I'm good with that. But where will you live?"

Silvia choked. Her hand went to the pain flooding her stomach. She hadn't gone there yet with any plan.

"You know I can't afford to pay this mortgage and rent you an apartment."

"You stay and I leave?" Blood rushed into her face, and her voice came out husky. She stood and walked a few paces to dissipate the stress.

"Let's face it," Frank said. "How could you even get to Unity House every day from here? Who would take care of the kids?"

She stopped and turned toward him, her mind numb. He kept on.

"No way will I allow them to move downtown; too much crime and terrible schools." Conviction rang in his voice. "I can sell the house and pay off the mortgage. The kids and I can move in with my mother. She's retired and can be there for them. She's amenable. They could be with you every weekend."

Whoa. Her breath quickened. They had worked out a plan, Frank and his mother. Just the two of them. The kids live with Tessa? No way, no way. Inside she screamed.

Then the dam broke. Guttural sobs shook her whole body.

With no hope for further negotiations, Frank sighed and climbed the stairs to the bedroom.

The next day Silvia arrived at Unity House with a headache and swollen red eyes. Sleep never happened. She wondered if her mood could climb out of its hellhole. If she was lucky, her eyes would shrink back to normal before anyone else came to the office.

Suddenly, her pain was forgotten. On top of the pile in her in-box was a draft proposal for funds with an attached note from John. *Please rewrite. It's your priority.*

Clarice's draft was full of platitudes and lacked sufficient detail to persuade any source of funds to support the cause. For the next few hours, Silvia added substance and made revisions, thankful that her skills were still needed. She gloated about the fact that Clarice wasn't a good writer.

It was after noon when John and Brad arrived. "Great news! Almost too good to be true." John's dimples showed fully in his broad smile. "George recruited another lawyer. Now there's two of them on this full time. And" – he put two thumbs up – "we got a commitment from a prestigious institute to statistically figure out which stations we should go after."

Silvia had good news to add. "This strategy, it's like a magnet; attracts folks with iron-clad commitment." She waited for their laughter, but they let her bad joke pass. "While you were away, a volunteer came by named Adam Reed. He's white; wore an expensive suit. Said he heard about the project from a Unitarian friend and will do anything. Of course I asked him if he could type. He laughed. He's young. Maybe he'd be good for research with you, Brad?"

John held up his hand. "Wait a minute. This one doesn't sit right with my gut. Let me check him out first. Did you have him fill out the form?"

She looked at the form and saw blank spaces where his work place and skill details were supposed to be. With eyes lowered, she handed him the form. "Sorry. I didn't even look at it."

John rolled his eyes. "Dear naïve one, was he good looking? Charming? Huh? Huh?" He pushed his face into hers, forcing eye contact. "You'd take the devil on as a volunteer, especially if he could type. It would be funny if it wasn't so dangerous."

As if he'd received a cue from the Almighty to take the stage, Elwood walked in the door. As usual, he jumped right into the conversation.

"Adam Reed's an undercover agent for the FBI." He directed a big smile at Silvia. "Maybe you could get J. Edgar on the volunteer roster?"

Confronted with her carelessness, Silvia groaned.

"Jesus," John said. "What the hell will we do with Adam Reed? That's all we need now – a fox in the hen house."

On the drive home and well into the night, Silvia forced herself to ponder the unthinkable. Some issues were fixed; not negotiable. She would not quit Unity House. She agreed about the bad schools and crime; the kids should not live downtown. Frank's income could not support two residences. Her parents were not available for child care as they were in and out of the country with their foreign service careers.

If she found a way to pay a lawyer, she could fight for full custody even though the black connection put her chance to win near zero. Forget that idea because no matter who won, a court fight would devastate everyone.

If she somehow was able to keep the house and the kids, transportation would be a problem. She would have to take a bus for two hours each way and borrow money from someone to pay a sitter to take care of them after school until she got home.

Finally, another crucial consideration, was Frank. He believed his children were his reason for being. She had no doubt he would suffer badly without them in his daily life.

Beads of perspiration trickled down her nose. Her shoulders were stiff; her neck ached. She got up from the couch where she slept since the divorce talks began and trudged into the kitchen for a towel to blot the sweat. Judas, the stove clock showed it was already 2 a.m. But *I have promises to keep and miles to go before I sleep.* The thought of Robert Frost's poem popping into her mind at that moment made her relax a little.

More buoyant, she fluffed up her pillow and lay on her back.

Maybe it wouldn't be so awful if she and the kids were only together on the weekends. They would play together – go to movies, ride bikes out to Mount Vernon, canoe on the canal. D.C. had great museums and parks and the glorious Potomac River. She could give the kids her full attention for two whole days. Such togetherness would be richer and fuller than the sporadic attention a mother can give in normal day-to-day living. Frank and his mother would have to do the daily stuff – provide discipline, help with homework, make sure they bathed and ate properly. The ache in her stomach lessoned. She sat up in hopes her brain would work better.

Then the ache came back at the thought of the kids with Tessa full time. Silvia had no doubt that Frank's mother loved her grandchildren and would take good care of their food, clothing and shelter. Some of her attitudes . . . God, they were so different from Silvia's. She would have to help the children feel compassion for their grandmother's limited view of life. And Tessa would receive innocent love from the children. Their presence would bring much-needed light to her dark side. When the kids came to Silvia every weekend, she would help them sort out any confusion; set them straight. Her role would shift from mother to more like that of a father. The parent who got to relax with the kids – play with them – at the end of a busy week.

She lay back down. Light began to mix in with the gloomy sorrow.

A week passed. Silvia was at Unity House, huddled around an audio tape player with John and Brad. The recorded conversation was between Harry Pine and Adam Reed. Harry had sent them the tape and explained they were in his office at CIA headquarters in McLean.

"I'm told you were sent in undercover to get involved in the black-directed project called Unity House on Capitol Hill. What are you supposed to be looking for?" asked Harry.

"You must be aware of Director Hoover's fear that black folks will try to take over the government. He even said, on the record, that if he were a black man living in America, he would join the Communist Party. So I'm supposed to be there to listen for any such un-American activities. And . . . um . . . I'm supposed to check on connections between Unity House and the Black Panthers. Why? What's the CIA's interest?"

There was a pause in the tape and what sounded like a chair scraping, as if someone needed to get more comfortable.

Harry's voice came on. "It's a personal interest. I'm a board member of Unity House. The Unitarian Churches in the area each have a member on the board. You can tell Director Hoover – actually, you need to tell your team leader – that while it's not the CIA's jurisdiction, we'll share anything that might be of interest to the FBI immediately. And I feel it's – um – it would be a mistake to try to infiltrate a church project. You know, freedom of religion and all that. There could be grounds for a government interference lawsuit, don't you think?"

Someone cleared his throat. "Okay, I hear you, Mr. Pine, sir. I'll be happy to take your – uh – suggestion back to my team leader. Frankly – off the record – I'd be happy to get back to my usual gig – out on the streets with the drugs and real crime. Tell me, how'd you know I was assigned there?"

"Sorry. I'm not at liberty to say."

The tape ended. John's smile was radiant, and so was Brad's. Silvia's heart swelled with love for whoever fixed her Adam Reed mistake.

At the end of her work day, Silvia stuck her head into John's office. "What's happened with Clarice? Is she still available for volunteer work?" She knew she was being catty but her lingering envy prevailed.

John looked up from his papers. "Ah, no. She's not available. She didn't pass the test."

Silvia started to pretend naïveté and ask what test. She stopped herself when she realized John would see through her ploy.

On the drive home, her attention stayed on the demise of Clarice. What a relief. She was glad until she noted a feeling twisted around her heart, like a snake. *Jealousy*. She had been slimed again by that enemy of her soul.

As the blossoms of spring morphed into summer's new greenery, vacation from school was in sight and the Nolan children filled the house with frenzied excitement. Silvia was glad for the high spirits that buffered the sorrow.

"How soon can you move out?" Frank's anger with Silvia was constant as time got closer to the actual separation. His words felt full of contempt when the kids weren't around, and when they were, he rarely spoke to her. She stopped herself from angry rebuttal which would have been her usual response. Instead she was propelled into a weird kind of detachment – a numbness – during the awful transition.

They had agreed to tell the kids Silvia had to move downtown to work on an important project. With their father, they would move to their grandmother's house during the week and be with their mother on the weekends. In their innocence, the kids never questioned the change. Instead, they looked forward to a new adventure.

"When is the house closing scheduled?" Silvia asked. She planned to move out in three weeks, if the sale of the house was completed.

"After the inspection. I hope the damn plumbing problem won't hang it up." Frank's furrowed brow and harsh tone conveyed his stress. "But don't expect any money from the sale. When the mortgage is paid off, the fees and commissions will eat up the surplus." He stared out the window into the back yard where the kids played. Then he angled toward Silvia but kept his eyes diverted. "How will you live?"

His question let her know that in addition to the pain of the separation, he suffered from his usual mistaken belief that he was inadequate as a financial provider. These self-doubts began soon after Frankie's birth and continued in spite of Silvia's efforts to diminish his fears. She believed most young families struggled to make ends meet and anyway, she was not longing for material wealth.

"You don't need to worry about me," she said. "We got the foundation grant and my stipend will cover living expenses. The friend I told you about, Carol, leased one of those old D.C. mansions that no single family can afford anymore. Five other people live there to share expenses. It's really cheap."

He didn't smile, but the deep lines in Frank's face smoothed a bit.

John assigned Silvia to organize and bring together the various aspects of the TV petition project. One element that continued to nag was the round-the-clock monitoring of the four Washington-area TV stations. At Jackie's suggestion, Silvia met with the head of the D.C. chapter of the welfare organization.

Mabel Williams, like many black women, had no signs of aging and was dressed in a green and white suit that complemented her plump figure. Her large smiling eyes and open demeanor gave her an attractive warmth. They chatted over coffee and shared stories about how they were drawn into their activist roles. When they got on topic, Silvia asked Mabel if, as Jackie had said, she really had more than one hundred women ready to do the TV monitoring.

Mabel's eyes lit up. "Indeed we do. We have more than two thousand members in the D.C. chapter already!"

"Mrs. Williams, do you – "

"Please call me Mabel." She put her hand on Silvia's arm.

Mabel obviously wanted Silvia to be more at ease. But Silvia's experience with volunteers taught that their commitment peaked and waned. Their motivation was not always strong enough to sustain itself when confronted with other uses for their time.

"Do you understand that there cannot be any breaks in the data? We have to constantly watch and log the programs from the time the stations sign on until sign off. We have to cover all the network channels. ABC, NBC, WRC plus WTTG. We will need teams of women day and night. If there are holes in our data, it could ruin our case. Do you understand?"

Mabel nodded. She agreed to a work session with Silvia to set up twenty-person teams for each station so no one had to be on duty too long. And if something came up where a scheduled watcher had to be away from the TV, they could easily switch times with another volunteer.

"Do you think a one-hour session to train the watchers will be enough?" Silvia asked.

"My word, it doesn't sound like that much work. Just watching TV and jotting down if there were any black folks on the air. We won't have to watch most of the shows. We already know there's nothing happening."

Silvia's stomach knotted; she gasped.

Mabel laughed and stuck her face in front of Silvia's. "I'm just messing with you." She patted Silvia's arm. "Relax, sister. We'll get this done."

Mabel had just left when John came out of his office to tell Brad and Silvia a visitor was coming from a prominent black organization. "His name is Ashton Judge. He was thrilled about the legal strategy to confront what he called D.C.'s white-on-white TV stations. He immediately took the plan to his membership for a vote to see if they wanted to participate. He said they jumped right in with no hesitation and no discussion. Their vote to get involved was instantly unanimous.

"Ashton is on his way over now to meet with me. I need you two to work in the back for a while until we get to know each other. A lot of black people we're gonna work with don't trust white folks being insiders on black-movement stuff. Already I've got to overcome their suspicions that I might be some stooge for the white man."

Both immediately grasped the situation, and closeted themselves in the conference room.

An hour later John asked Brad and Silvia to return to the front room. "I want you to hear this." A cheerful sense of urgency colored his voice. "Ashton, tell them what you just told me."

"Our group . . . it's a coalition made up of all the relevant black groups in D.C., so our members are the leaders of these organizations. They're the niggers the stations are supposed to have interviewed to find out what their people wanted to see on TV. After what brother John told me – about challenging the MF's assessment of community needs – well, I'll bet not a one of our membership was interviewed. Who knew it was against the law for those boys to only broadcast what white people wanna see? Well, now we know, and we want law and order!"

Ashton stood, put his left hand on his hip, and with his right pretended to draw a gun from an invisible shoulder holster. He pointed his finger into the air. "*Pow, pow, pow!* We got 'em cold."

Everyone howled.

Ashton was a jolly fellow in his early forties, chunky, with dark-rimmed glasses and an Afro hairstyle. He wore a suit and tie. He told the group he worked for IBM, and had for twenty years. He knew to trust some white people and others not so much. He pointed out this trust factor was the same with black folks. Some, yes, but not all. When he first heard about John's project, funded by a white church with white people on the board, he wondered if John was an Uncle Tom. "But John's real. Any dude who worked the streets before moving up has the right experience in my book."

John grinned throughout Ashton's report.

Silvia was thrilled with the enormous strength Ashton's group would bring to their petition. So was Brad, whose usual stoic and skeptical expression had changed to a broad smile. He asked Ashton if he thought his members would sign affidavits attesting to not being interviewed.

"Those niggers will not just sign, they'll show up in person and give sworn testimony."

Ashton's sense of humor triggered Silvia's. "How come you all can call each other the N word and we can't?"

Ashton laughed. "Just because, white girl. Just because."

John chuckled. "It takes one to know one, and you ain't one."

When Ashton was gone, John gave Silvia and Brad more insights into some of the current black attitudes. "You can't know how much you don't know about our real down-home – when we're on the streets face-to-face – culture. But I can tell you one thing. We're so down on each other that most blacks don't believe their own people can put together any legal petition against a big TV station. So the niggers are gonna be looking for who are the white people behind this. The truth is this is a black strategy. It's happening because of a whole group of black people, beginning with a young black lawyer in Mississippi who got us standing in court. And yes, we'll use white folks like yourselves and George Hardy, and the church groups, and so on. But this is a black-directed project and we will get this done."

"Amen. Glory Alleluia!" Silvia thrust her hands into the air.

"Yes, indeed, this will get done!" Brad said.

Elwood walked in and joined the chorus. "Yes, we will!"

A great and cheerful sense of triumph radiated through Unity House.

But that night as she tried for sleep, Silvia worried that maybe their optimism was too high – everything was going too well. Maybe they were being set-up to such great heights for a very great fall.

The weeks sped by and moving day arrived. Silvia showed the kids what they could carry out to the car. "Just this suitcase and those boxes."

On the drive downtown, they chatted cheerfully about the great adventures in store.

"The house where I'll be living is near the Lincoln Memorial, so we'll go by and wave to Abe." Everyone loved the memorial. The kids because of the steep stairs to run up and down and the multiple columns to hide behind; Silvia because there she could feel Abe Lincoln's beautiful soul.

After Frank and the kids drove out of sight, grief swamped Silvia's entire being. Arms, legs – everything trembled. None of her housemates were home, so she quickly moved her stuff into her room, threw herself on the empty bed and surrendered to convulsive sobs. She didn't know how much time passed, but it had been daylight when she arrived and when she was ready to get up, it was dark. Her body felt like it had been pummeled. Unfamiliar sounds of city traffic flooded her ears as it whooshed by the busy street that fronted the house. The voices of men and women talking and laughing rose up from the floor below. It sounded like a party.

Grateful for company, she forced herself out of her malaise, washed her face with cold water and went downstairs.

Carol smiled when she saw her friend and hugged her with such warmth, a smile pushed through Silvia's swollen eyes. Her roommate, Marilyn, welcomed her with a beer and they joined the crowd.

After a few drinks, Silvia slipped away and for the rest of the night, feigned sleep until the first sign of daylight. Then she walked the five blocks to Unity House.

It was 6 a.m. when she stepped through the red door. Right away the revered work consumed her mind and dissipated the stress of the past twenty-four hours. She was glad to have time without interruption to finish the report of Unity House activities for the board.

When John arrived at nine, he was surprised. "My God! Have you been here all weekend?"

"Good morning." She cupped her chin in her hand and eyed him with a sly grin. "Some of us are seriously committed. Others just laze around all weekend."

"Is that so?" He laughed as he put down his briefcase and perched on the edge of her desk. "Well, here you are. You've moved into Unity House." The warmth in his eyes and voice eased some of her separation grief.

"Yes. I'm home." Exposed. Her hands flew to cover her mouth. She'd just out-ed her secret feeling about Unity House.

But for John it had never been a secret. Silvia bonded with the project her first day. He hopped up and waved his fists in the air. "Right on! There will be no stopping us now." He smiled and danced happily into his office. Then he danced back out and asked if she was all settled in or did she need his help to unpack?

The thought of John involved in those types of details made her laugh out loud. "Nope, but thanks for the offer. I'm good."

The phone rang. John took it in his office; Silvia went back to work.

At ten, Brad arrived. "So, how did it go with the kids?" He picked up the new photo she'd placed on her desk and admired the three beaming children. She had shared some of the details of the split with Brad, so he was aware of what she was going through. She told him they were fine since they thought of her move as temporary. "Just until racism's over," Frankie had said.

Through their laughter, Brad spoke. "Well, you know, for his generation the end could be in sight."

"Let us pray," Silvia said. "Maybe our great, great grand-children will study racism as ancient history."

She lost herself in the day's work until late afternoon, when Ashton came racing through the door. "Have I got news!"

Everyone hurried to hear what he had to say.

"We got the name of our media challenge group. You'll never guess. Never. It's too good."

"Okay, okay, spill it," John said.

"*B* period, *E* period, *S* period, *T* period. That's the name." Ashton grinned and pranced around the room. "But guess what it stands for?"

Silvia was game. "Um . . . better – business – black – escapades. No, I give up." No one else even tried.

"Come on, man, just tell us," John said.

"Black Efforts for Soul in Television."

While the words sunk in, everybody stayed silent.

Silvia was the first to speak. "My God, it's perfect!"

Brad gave two thumbs up.

"That's exactly what we're doing. Who came up with this?" John asked.

"My *wife*. We all sat for hours, working our brains. Nothing we came up with seemed good enough. She came in to serve drinks and heard our struggle. The name just flowed out of her. She told us to just tell it like it is. Simple."

The group's elation stopped abruptly when a man no one knew came in the front door. He looked around for a moment. "Sorry to interrupt. Name's Ralph Ziegler. I write for *Broadcasting Magazine*." He thrust his hand toward John, who hesitated a moment and then shook it.

"*Broadcasting Magazine*?" John asked.

The others looked on wide-eyed. Ziegler was a small man, white, in his early fifties, with blue eyes and a friendly open face. His tie was loose and he carried his jacket over his shoulder.

He chuckled. "You all look like the enemy's in the room, but it's not like that. Yes, the magazine is the industry's news source, but we let them know what they need to be worried about. Rumor has it you folks plan to file a petition-to-deny license renewal against some TV station in this city and maybe others. Am I right? Is this the place?"

John's caution put him on guard. "Let's go to my office, Mr. Ziegler – did I get that right?" John ushered him in and closed the door.

Ashton, Brad and Silvia went back to the conference room. Silvia was pleased. "If this guy is for real, this could be a great help for us. The broadcasters will start to change their ways before we even file; they'll want to get out in front of it."

"On the other hand, these MF white boys most probably will react warlike and do everything in their power to stop us before we can file the first petition. These MFs aren't as nice as you, girl. And if they're scared – and they will be because a fight will cost them money – they'll have to pay lawyers to respond to our petitions."

"I'm with him," Brad said. "It makes me nervous for them to know this far ahead of time. We've got months until deadline. That's plenty of time to do damage."

Silvia thought over their concerns. "Okay, war boys. If you were them, what kind of dirty tricks would you try? What should we be prepared to protect ourselves from? Our phones are already tapped. Our plan is for a legal war, right? Paper and reason are our weapons, yes?" She looked at Ashton. "Unless there's something going on I don't know about."

Ashton looked up at the ceiling, then at her. "I'm not at liberty to say."

What? She was about to get upset until she saw Ashton's grin. "If there was something going on, it sure wouldn't happen out of this office. And you, Miss Trusting of Everyone, even the devil, would be the last to know."

Silvia laughed at the label. "It's my greatest defense. Someday you'll be as wise as me."

Ashton opened his mouth to retort but stopped when the front door shut with its usual loud smack. Everyone moved quickly to join John.

"He says he won't publish the story until we file. He wanted to know which station we're going to hit. I told him the truth, that it might be all of them, but even we won't know until the research is finished. I let him know we have this vast army on our side. I named them – Citizens Communication Center, Urban Law Institute, United Church of Christ, Institute for Policy Studies. Wanted him to know there was no doubt we were capable."

"Did you tell him about B.E.S.T.?" Ashton asked.

"Hell no. We should wait to scare them when we formally release it to the press. Your boys plan to do that, right?"

"Yes, I'm supposed to draft the statement since I'm head of communications. I'll do it tonight. I've got to get back to work now."

"I'll do some checks on Ralph and *Broadcasting Magazine*." John looked relaxed. "My gut tells me he's a genuine human being. But if he found out about our plan through rumor, we can bet the TV stations already know it's in the works. They'll try to stop it before it gets filed."

Elwood walked in with his big smile. He held out his hand to Ashton. "I'm Elwood. Sort of a fixture around here."

John took over. "Ashton, the truth is . . . Elwood's the Unity House guru. He takes care of us."

Ashton smiled and did the brother's handshake with Elwood. "Always happy to be on the right side of the Lord."

Silvia wondered what brought Elwood in this time. Did he have something on Ralph or what? She gave him a sideways look. He winked. Then he pulled a small tape recorder out of his jacket pocket and stood it on the table. "What you're about to hear is a meeting of TV stations managers called by a communications lawyer who is retained by several of them. The first voice you'll hear is the lawyer."

First voice: "It's led by a black guy. John Darnell. He's directing a project called Unity House, funded by a consortium of churches. Whether or not it's tied to groups like the Black Panthers we don't know yet. The FBI has eyes on it. We don't know if they plan to hit all the TV stations at once or single out just one. But I'll tell you, it could get real messy. Who knows what that son of a bitch Nick Johnson will come out with next. He's already got the niggers all puffed up the way he blames the media for the riots."

Second voice: "Who's doing the legal work?"

First voice: "A lone-wolf attorney funded by a not-for-profit he set up. He's Stanford Law. A white guy. Definitely on the attack. But he's single. I don't see any vulnerability there."

Third voice: "What about this John guy – is he vulnerable? Somebody who might turn around if we found some dirt on him?"

First voice: "Not likely since his past is out in the open. He raised himself up off the streets. Was actually a pimp. He did a stint in the Air Force and then into legitimate business. There is a white woman who works close with him. I hear she has some kids and a husband in the suburbs. Maybe she could be turned. I'll check it out."

The tape ended there. Silvia's heart beat faster; all eyes went to her. "So I guess . . . uh . . . I'm famous." Everyone looked uneasy.

"Don't worry about her," Elwood said. "She's clean as a whistle. Even if they dug up something, she'd invite them to expose it. She'd never turn."

Elwood flashed a smile at Silvia. She relaxed a little.

"How'd you get that recording?" Brad asked.

"I have my spies. Of course, they're usually invisible to ordinary humans." Elwood grinned. "But when I need material evidence, it takes a hardware device. Good thing this meeting was in a golf club dining room. Easy access."

Anxiety about a possible attack from the TV people began to arise in Silvia's mind. Her imagination flared; what if they tried to harm her children?

On Saturday, Silvia was up before sunrise. She was ecstatic. The kids were coming! Even though they talked on the phone every night since the move, their sweet voices had only made her miss them more.

She checked in the kitchen to make sure she hadn't forgotten any of their favorite foods – hot dogs, potatoes for homemade French fries, carrots, spinach, apples, peanut butter, chocolate chip cookies, French toast bread, maple syrup, butter, Cheerios, eggs, orange juice and milk. Ice cream would be picked up when they were together so the kids could choose flavors.

She planned to spoil them rotten, but only for the first visit. Luckily, her room-mate had gone to visit her parents for the weekend, so they could all sleep in the same room. And joy of all joys, the Smithsonian Folk Life Festival was in full swing – tents, rides for the kids, live musicians, exhibits they could touch and endless food.

Frank wouldn't look her in the eyes when he dropped them off, but the kids bounced with excitement. They hugged and kissed their mother and proudly showed the treasures they brought in their overnight bags.

"I'll be back Sunday at four to pick them up." The sternness in Frank's voice revealed that his resentment stayed strong. In the past Silvia would have been hurt by his I'm-not-speaking-to-nor-looking-at-you treatment. But now – with distance between them – his attitude seemed more harmful to him than to her.

The festival proved to be a rich experience for everyone. Tents, decorated with balloons and colorful flags filled the National Mall. The July day was sunny yet blissfully free of the high humidity that usually cloaked D.C.in sweaty air.

The kids watched a Choctaw woman weave baskets out of river cane and were thrilled when she allowed them to weave small mats out of her supply. Silvia enjoyed watching her children so fully engaged until something pulled her attention away.

What she saw made her go into high alert.

A man, who stood at the tent entrance, stared at her with such force she felt assaulted by invisible rays of cruelty. The moment he knew she spotted him, he tore out of the tent like a darting lizard.

Oh God. Silvia's legs trembled. Her panic was for Frankie, Linda and Alan. Fear snapped into anger; the type a tiger mother feels when anyone or anything threatens her children. No way should any harm, even an ugly look from some geezer, come to them. This man could be part of some pushback against the petition strategy. No matter what, she was a warrior, poised for battle.

For the remainder of the weekend she was on watch duty for anyone who looked suspicious.

4

One month passed and D.C. sweltered under the ninety-degree humidity, characteristic of the swampland it was before it was drained to become the Nation's capital. Silvia forgot about the *bogeyman caper*, nick-named by John and Brad who joked that she mistook a lewd man admiring her good looks for a spy. As Silvia began her walk to Unity House – she loved being able to walk to work – two professionally groomed men with somber faces approached. They stopped and stood shoulder to shoulder to block her way forward. IDs were thrust in her face. FBI. Fear turned to indignation when she recognized one of them. The *bogeyman*! She gave them a mean stare and faked a calm demeanor, a skill mastered from years of motherhood. She decided to keep quiet about seeing the agent at the festival.

"Okay, FBI boys, how can I help you?" They were about her age, one taller than the other, both white, with crew cuts and wiry bodies in polyester suits. They continued looking stern.

"We want to talk to you at our offices." Agent One, the bogeyman, kept a sober face as he indicated the car parked at the curb.

"Sorry, I have to get to work."

"We'll drive you to work. You can tell your boss you need to be excused for an hour or so," said Agent Two.

No way would she get into a car with these guys. "Let's talk here. No one's around to listen."

They changed strategy and put on smiles. "How about you come to our office when it's more convenient for you," said Agent Two. "Here's my card. Give me a call when you're ready to come so we're sure to be there. We're in the FBI head-quarters in the Department of Justice building. My name's Fred Alexander and this here's Jeremy Franklin."

"What's this about?"

"Routine matter," said Agent One. "We'll tell you when you have time. But you better have time soon. Don't make us come after you." He shook his finger, bolstering the threat.

Obnoxious boys, they love to show off their power. "I'll call you." Her tone was surly.

She hurried to Unity House and went directly to John's office. He was busy and didn't look up.

"I was stopped by two FBI agents on the way over."

He frowned and gave his full attention.

"They wanted me to get in their car and go to their office. Who would do that?"

He looked wide-eyed. "Go on."

"So they gave me their cards and said I should call and make an appointment. 'And soon,' they said, or they'd come and get me. And guess what else?" Impatiently, John waved his hand for her to continue. "One of them is the bogeyman." Silvia smothered her desire to poke John for not believing her.

His eyes clouded. "Let's get Elwood in to check this out. It smells bad."

"What do you think they want with me?"

"No doubt they want to know what you're doing with black folks. They probably want to turn you away from us. Make you their spy."

She laughed at the absurdity of the idea. "Oh, is that all. Um . . . I could be a double agent."

John didn't laugh and remained quiet until Elwood arrived in his usual mysterious way.

"They've heard about the plan to mess with the TV stations and want to find a weak link to become an informant. The FBI doesn't like to deal with surprises." Elwood stood quietly with his eyes closed for some time. "They might try to blackmail you, Silvia. Have you done anything you would not want anyone to know about, including husband, children, parents, siblings or anyone else you can think of?"

Silvia considered her secrets. Her thoughts went to the time she lost her virginity; before marriage. That was all she could think of. Embarrassing? Yes. Would she betray this work to keep such a thing quiet? The notion was ridiculous. Also, she was relieved that the bogeyman was FBI instead of some criminal hired to hurt her children. "I think I should go and let them interrogate me. It would be good to find out where they're coming from," she said.

Elwood closed his eyes again. When he emerged, he advised that she should go. "What they ask will give us an insider view of the FBI mentality, yet will do no harm to Unity House."

John still looked troubled. "Okay, but only if we wire her with a tape recorder, FBI-style. That way we'll have evidence of abuse if it goes wrong."

Inside interrogation room B4, Fred, the good cop, was asking about the coed house where Silvia lived.

"So there are three guys and three women living together in this house. Are you just friends? Does everyone have their own bedroom?"

With her heart pounding, Silvia struggled to maintain composure and not scratch the itch she felt from the tape used to plaster the wire to her chest. She was appalled when her words came out jerky. "Yes…and… and no. I….I share a room with another woman." She paused to gain better control of her voice. "It keeps our rent low cause we're doing the work we believe needs doing, with low pay. The rest of the housemates have their own rooms."

"So who's your roommate? What's her name – Marilyn?"

Silvia nodded, wondering how they knew.

"She works at Unity House with you?"

Her nervousness dialed down when she realized they didn't know everything. "No, she's working to save the environment."

"So is everyone living in this house working on some cause?"

Why were they so interested in the goings-on at the house? Silvia paused, pondering their motives; then decided it wouldn't harm anyone for her to answer truthfully. "Two work on the Vietnam thing. One guy is a Native American lawyer working to right the wrongs against his people. Another works at a not-for-profit that builds affordable housing."

Silvia decided it was time to show some impatience with their line of questioning. "What does all this have to do with me? I didn't know any of my housemates before moving in except for Carol, who manages the rental. She didn't know any of them before either. She put ads in the classifieds to find renters. They're all good people. Everything they're doing is out in the open. No one's wants to overthrow the government. Just want to persuade policy-makers to improve things."

Jeremy, the bad cop, stepped in to continue the questioning. "I don't believe men and women who live together in the same house don't have sex going on." His voice changed to a drawl. "What do you do, switch around every night? Or is it boys with boys and girls with girls?" Abruptly his voice grew harsh. "I want the truth about what goes on there!"

Silvia let this revelation about the FBI mindset soak in. Then, with a sly smile, she could not let the opportunity pass by. "Interesting. You don't believe men and women who are not married can live in the same house without having sex? When you grew up in a family, did you sleep with your sisters?" She gave them her I'm-ashamed-of-you look. "It's a sad situation when FBI agents, who often decide who our enemies are, can't understand the concept that we're all sisters and brothers. What are you, some kind of sex maniacs?"

Jeremy scowled angrily. "You better watch what you say, missy. We can shut you down anytime we want. Your arrogance can be very, very dangerous. Not just for you, but for your family and friends."

Fred took over. "All right, that's enough for today. Mrs. Nolan, you can go now."

Her legs trembled as she sped out of the building. God, did she just set off the wrath of the FBI? Her heart resumed its loud thumping; her breath quickened. To shake off stress, she decided to hike the few miles back to Unity House. Her skin inside her blouse was being scraped by the tape recorder but she didn't dare stop to remove it. What if they were watching? She pounded the sidewalk, increasing speed to keep up with her racing thoughts. Oh God. Oh God. Would they really hurt her family? They could mess with her father's government job. They could shut down Unity House. Tears rolled down her face and she was wet all over with perspiration.

John, Brad and Lisa, the new secretary, huddled over the playback of Silvia's FBI encounter as she watched helplessly. They exchanged surprised looks when it became clear that the FBI wasn't interested in Unity House, only in Silvia's politically active housemates. Brad remarked that apparently Unity House activities were in the open enough to be dismissed as no threat to domestic security.

But her brazen remarks about the sexual mindset of the FBI put fear into John.

"Black people have been killed by the FBI for *no goddamn reason* and you go being a loud mouth. You set up bad blood between Unity House and the FBI. Didn't you think about the fact that you represented Unity House? You just had to insult those guys. You could have just told them you didn't indulge and let it go at that. But oh no, Miss I'll-show-you-how-clever-I-am. You just had to ding them."

John's words hit Silvia like bullets. "Oh my God, I'm so, so sorry – "

He held up his hand. "Don't speak. Take some time and dwell on what harm you might have caused." He strode into his office and slammed the door.

Lisa and Brad kept blank looks and resumed their work. Silvia's face burned and her body continued to tremble. Usually she cried when chastised, but this time her angst went beyond tears. She sat at her desk, lit a cigarette and stared at the typewriter. God, such stupid carelessness. What was her problem? Ego? God, please make it better.

In desperation, she turned to Lisa. "Any advice?"

The two women had quickly become friends when Lisa joined Unity House. They were the same age, married – or had been married – with children. Lisa was black and beautiful with a trim Afro that accentuated her full lips and deep brown eyes. She had a dry humor that matched her Southern drawl. Her commitment to the Unity House cause reflected in her actions – she did whatever was necessary to get the work done.

Lisa gently nudged Silvia to a standing position and turned her toward the door. "You take another walk until you're less tense. Then come back."

Silvia mustered a grateful nod and hit the sidewalk at a fast clip. Excruciating emotions blocked her mind's ability to sort things out. One block, then two, then three until she found herself on the Capitol grounds. She sat on a bench and let nature pull her attention to the beauty of the huge maple trees. Their leaves were still lush and green; not ready yet to face Fall's recycling. The blessed sun blazed warmth on her back, soothing away tension. She walked back at a slower pace but upset continued to weigh heavily on her heart.

As soon the door smacked shut behind her, Silvia was summoned to John's office. He closed the door. She sat stiffly, terrified of losing the job that fulfilled so much of her life's purpose.

"Relax, girl. It's not like you committed an unforgiveable sin. I'm your friend, so I'm going to define a problem I see in you so you can fix it. Your problem could put us all in danger." He paused and studied her as if to make sure she was calm enough to listen. She took a deep breath, but stayed rigidly on the edge of her seat.

"Okay, here's what I see. If we put it into one word, the word is 'uppity;' my grandmother's term for 'fresh' or 'cocky' or 'cheeky.' In other words, when some-one strikes you the wrong way, no matter who it is, you get up on your high horse and charge into combat." He paused to allow what he said to sink in.

She relaxed a little. He wasn't going to fire her? But, oh God, what he said was true. In her family, the women fought a lot. It was psychological warfare. She could give a snappy rebut to any argument or insult in a second. She had years of training.

John had more to say. "That type of flippant response is dangerous. Slavery taught us to be extremely cautious dealing with authority, especially the white man. I'm sure you know they'd kill us on the spot. Hang us. Put a bullet through our head. Burn crosses on our lawns. We were taught by every black person in our community – not just our parents and grandparents, but everybody – to never react in front of a white man. It's a kind of patience that's required for survival; one handed down over generations. We only allow our reactions to be seen by each other."

He moved closer, his eyes drilling into hers. "If the law is pissed off at you, they'll put you in jail just for smoking a joint – you know that, don't you? Maybe we should let the FBI throw you in jail. Give you some time to churn on what makes you have to be a smart mouth."

She had been so scared he would fire her that jail sounded better. Yet no way would she say that out loud. "I don't want to go to jail. Please . . . I understand what you said. I do react knee-jerk. I . . . I realize I am dangerous. Also stupid. I do want to unlearn being uppity." Her face was contorted, her voice shrill. "I just pray there's no backlash from the FBI."

"Well, keep praying and wash your mouth out with soap." John laughed and spoke compassionately. "Lighten up, girl. It's not the end of the world."

On Saturday morning, Silvia borrowed a housemate's car to drive to the suburbs to watch the kids play soccer. After a rough week, she was eager for the comfort of their unconditional love. Alan's game was already underway when she arrived, so she hurried to meet up with her family.

As soon as they saw her, Frankie and Linda deliberately looked away without a greeting. Oh God, it was the silent treatment. The hurt felt like a punch in her stomach. Inside she wailed. Frank has infected the kids. Fear of losing their love gripped her heart.

For the next fifteen minutes, she stood on the sidelines and pretended to watch the game while she fought to keep the tears at bay. Think positive. Think positive. She doubted Frank and Tessa told them in words to snub her. Maybe the kids were simply echoing their father's behavior. She pulled herself out of remorse and began to cheer for Alan's team. As her mood improved, Frankie and Linda moved beside her. Linda put her arm around Silvia's waist. Frankie asked if she could stay for his game too.

"Of course. That's why I'm here." Overwhelmed with relief, she hugged and kissed her children.

In spite of Frank's continued aloofness, Silvia moved closer and delicately asked if she could take them all out for dinner after the games.

"No, dinner's being cooked at home. Maybe some other time." Frank stalked away.

Anger rose up but she pushed it away to keep the little time she had left with the kids upbeat. No doubt his contempt hid a deep hurt. And she was the cause. Frank had a stubborn mindset when someone had wronged him. His attitude could cause the kids to feel like they should be loyal to him and be mad at her too.

When the games were over and the loaded car drove out of the parking lot, Frankie shouted out the open window, "Mommy, when are you coming home?" They were too far away to hear, so she held up her palms and shrugged. It seemed unlikely that she and Frank would ever get back together as husband and wife.

"Wow!" Silvia cheered loudly as she hung up the phone. John hurried out of his office and Lisa looked up from her work. "It's amazing how fast everyone buys into this strategy. I contacted the guys you gave me in Chicago, Dallas and St. Louis. I'm only on the phone for ten minutes before they ask for the workshops and any other how-to-do-it guidelines. They want everything right away. The Chicago guy asked if we could come out tomorrow and get them started." She threw her fists up as if celebrating a touchdown.

"Beautiful. That's what I knew would happen. If black groups file petitions against TV stations all over the country at about the same time, it will look like we're a huge organization. Silvia, can you and Lisa put together a draft of the guidelines today?"

"Of course," they said in unison.

"Good. I'll get you a list of contacts in every major city. We'll phone them first with the plan and airmail the packages."

The team was humming along, happily working towards what appeared to be certain victory, when the phone rang. It was Mabel Williams. She skipped the small talk and told Silvia right out that there was one eight-hour segment of TV monitoring missing.

Silvia's mind raced into panic. It was too late now to fill in the gap. Her mouth went dry. She took a deep breath and croaked, "How did it happen?"

"Trinity had family problems and couldn't get to it," Mabel tried to sound matter-of-fact but Silvia knew she was rattled as her usual cheerful tone was gone.

"But we had backup for her; we had backup for everyone." Silvia's fear flooded her throat. "What the hell happened?"

"She didn't let her backup know."

When John heard the news, he immediately called George. Silvia, on the extension, listened in anguish. George was silent for what seemed like ages. Then he spoke slowly. "Um, could be deadly serious if the FCC decided our allegations raised enough doubts that they'd have to hold hearings. But I won't lie to you – they have never held hearings for anyone's license renewal accept when they suspected outright fraud." He paused again. "Even in the unlikely event they did hold hearings, I think we could fill in the gap with the stations' own program logs." His voice got lighter. "We'll work it out. No need to collapse over this."

What? Did he mean this breach in the data wasn't such a big problem after all? She felt stupid to have spent so much time and energy in a worried state for fear of data breaches. She immediately called Mabel, gave her the good news, and apologized for the pressure she had laid on her. Good natured Mabel, of course, forgave instantly.

As the deadline got closer, tension increased and cluttered Silvia's usual clear focus. Sleep, when it came, was clogged with thorny nonsensical dreams. Her face broke out in blemishes thanks to endless cups of coffee, cigarettes and pizza consumed on the run. Still, there was no time to slack off.

With one week to go, Silvia and Lisa agreed to meet at the office at 6 a.m. to organize the hundreds of pages of appendices to the petition. When Silvia arrived, the door was slightly ajar. That was odd.

Cautiously, she stepped inside. Strewn around the floor was a pile of debris – pens, papers, rubber bands. Fear clutched her chest. She slowly backed away, but too late. Two burly arms grabbed her from behind. A large strong hand grasped both her wrists and pinned them behind her back while the other waved a knife in front of her face. With all her strength she lunged forward, but was jerked back with such force she shrieked. With his knife hand, he covered her mouth while he pulled and yanked her down the hall.

Her assailant was a burly black man with a bandanna tied around his head to hide his nose and mouth. He was rough and confident; a professional criminal and she was no match.

Inside the conference room another black man with his nose and mouth covered, paced nervously around the room. What she saw next slammed her into deeper shock.

There was Lisa, naked, gagged, hands tied behind her back, eyes closed, lying face down on the floor. Dead?

Before Silvia could scream, Lisa turned her head. She was alive!

Racked with fear, Silvia managed to calmly lie. "Two men will be here any minute for a meeting."

"Shut up!" The knifeman snarled. "Take off your clothes."

Horrified, her cold hands trembled while she removed each garment. With fierce swipes of his razor sharp knife he slashed them into strips which he used as rope to gag her mouth and tie her hands behind her back.

He shoved her with his knee and spoke gruffly. "Move! Get face down on the floor."

Oh God, help! She screamed inside herself as he yanked her down and tied her ankles together. Several times his bandana slipped off but each time she instinctively shut her eyes so he wouldn't fear she'd recognize him – if she lived. He kept up his fear tactics and turned her face so she could watch him dump her purse on the floor and put her wallet in the pocket of his military-style jacket. Then he jerked off her rings and watch with such force her fingers ached.

His booty collected, he stood still and Silvia felt him eyeing her nakedness.

"Mmm . . ." His tone shifted. "You must be one of them white girls who loves it. Tell me, baby, do you have a boyfriend?" His voice was low and in a tone he probably thought was sensuous. "Did you have sex last night?"

Thanks to God, John had taught her the protocols of street sex life. She knew exactly why he wanted this information. She nodded *yes*, moving her head up and down multiple times so there would be no doubt about the answer.

Now his tone was matter-of-fact. "And did you wash yourself after?"

She turned her head from side to side; a definite *no*.

"What kind of woman are you?" he scolded. In prostitute-speak, it was a mortal sin not to wash thoroughly between tricks. If she hadn't been so terrified, she would have laughed at his audacity to condemn her while *he* was performing an immoral, felony assault.

Before knifeman could go any further, his less confident partner – who had never stopped his nervous trot up the hallway and back – made an urgent request. "Let's get out of here before someone else comes. Let's go!" With that, the two thugs hurried out and slammed the front door.

The women lay still and listened to make sure the terrorists had gone. They twisted and scooted towards each other. With their teeth, they tore their gags aside and untied each other's wrist bindings. While they worked to free themselves, they spoke in hushed tones in case the bad guys lingered.

The only items available to cover their nudity were two pairs of burlap curtains that covered the windows. With strong tugs that broke the rods, they pulled them down and wrapped themselves. The material was rough and scratchy and had to be belted with pieces of their shredded clothes to keep them on. But grateful for the cover-up, they hurried to the front, bolted the door and called the police.

While they waited, their continued trembling did not stop them from making fun of their attackers.

"That thug giving you a lecture on cleanliness … unbelievable!" Lisa laughed. "And I told the exact same lie about men coming for a meeting. That might have been what saved us. And when they slashed my clothes before you came, I asked them why. They said it was so we wouldn't run after them. Can you believe it?"

They hooted loudly at this idea and agreed that even if they'd been fully clothed and had machine guns, they would let someone trained to capture bad guys do the job.

With blaring sirens and flashing red lights, three police cars responded. At the same time, John arrived. Color drained from his face when he saw Lisa and Silvia clothed in the conference room curtains. Pain lined his face while he listened with the four policemen and two detectives as the women told the story of their abduction.

John's body stiffened; his hands fisted. "Some son-of-a-bitch hired these god damn thugs to sabotage the petition strategy." He banged his fist on the desk.

The detectives questioned all three about their personal lives and the Unity House work. The police dusted for fingerprints and looked for other evidence. All the desk drawers had been pulled out and dumped. Thankfully, the file drawers and stacks of papers readied for the petition were left intact. The police surmised they were looking for valuables that could easily be fenced. Maybe they had drug habits to support.

Lisa telephoned her husband, and Silvia called Carol. They soon arrived with sympathy and clothes so Silvia and Lisa could go to the police station to look at mug shots. A highly agitated John insisted on going along.

Within an hour, both women identified the knifeman. Leo Nathaniel Franklin was thirty-five and had been in and out of prison most of his life for various felonies, including sexual assault. Silvia swallowed hard, grateful to have been spared.

When John heard the criminal's name, he swore under his breath, leapt to his feet and moved beside the detective to see the photo. His voice was raspy. "Yep, that's Leo. He was a pimp when I was. We fought over broads and territory. This is payback, I'm sure of it! That son of a bitch. Bastard! I'll tell you where you might find him." The scowl on his face darkened his complexion.

"We've got his parole officer on the phone now," one of the detectives said. "He says Leo escaped from a halfway house – he's got to be in the area. No car, no money, no passport. I'll take what you've got, just give us a few days." The detective sounded confident.

Sure enough, the cops were good. A few days later, Lisa and Silvia identified Leo in a lineup. The detective told them Leo confessed. He knew he was going back to prison and would receive better treatment if he cooperated so gave the name of his accomplice and address of his hideout. Silvia and Lisa praised the officers for their speedy resolution. But John remained deeply troubled about a possible conspiracy.

In an attempt to put John at ease, the detectives invited the threesome to listen to parts of Leo's interrogation. Silvia's body stiffened when she heard Leo's voice. A wave of nausea touched her throat; she swallowed it down so as not to miss a word.

The detective asked Leo if he knew John Darnell

"Yep, I know him. What of it?"

"Did you know it was his office you messed with?"

No answer.

"Well?"

"Yep, I knew what I was doing. So what?"

"Why'd you choose his place? You're a pro. You knew you weren't going to find expensive jewelry or money under a mattress."

"I hate that dude. He's nothing but a pimp. I heard some counselor woman tell her friends what a hero he was." He pitched his voice high to mimic the counselor. "'John Darnell's a saint. He's got white folks working for him to get us our comeuppance.' What a crock of shit."

"Why do you hate him so much?"

"Back in the day we worked the same streets. When I had a broad that was going good, it never failed. He lured her away from me."

"How did he do that?"

"He had this spooky vibe; pissed me off. Sweet talk, money, who knows? They just kept leaving me."

"So this was revenge. Why did you hit on the women?"

"I was going to break in, tear it up, and take anything that looked good. When we reached the place, a woman was at the door with a key. We rushed in behind her. Soon after the first woman, another walked in. Those broads were a bonus."

"A bonus?" Silvia and Lisa shrieked in unison.

"I hope he burns in hell." Lisa banged her fist on the table.

Gloom swamped over Silvia. Why did this happen to them? If only they had not gone to work early, they would have arrived after a robbery. They could have escaped the pain from being manhandled by these thugs.

With the petition deadline less than a week away, Lisa and Silvia sought Elwood's help to rid themselves of the added layers of stress from the assault. Upon his arrival, he tipped his handsome fedora to the ladies and guided them directly to the room they had been avoiding – the conference room.

Inside the scene of the crime, Silvia's hands became clammy, her throat dry. New curtains hung on the windows and the room had been scrubbed by professional cleaners. John had new double bolt locks put on all the windows and doors. Still, she and Lisa sat perspiring, shoulders hunched.

Elwood asked them to close their eyes and notice what physical sensations they felt inside and out. Silvia's stomach was in turmoil as her mind replayed the assault: a masked Leo grabbed and slashed; the knife cold against her throat; her body jerked and yanked, pushed and pulled; clothing hacked; Lisa naked, tied and gagged; boots clomped; the door slammed.

It seemed like hours for the replay of the assault to fade. Finally Silvia felt a subtle, bubbling field of energy that seemed to encase her like a cocoon. The vibrations massaged her face – eyes, nose, forehead, throat. Everywhere. She felt it work its way deeper inside as it soothed and relaxed tensions.

Elwood asked, "Where is the fear now?"

"Gone," Silvia said.

"Yes," Lisa said. "Gone."

"Okay. Have you ever faced your fear of death?"

"No," Silvia said.

"Yes," Lisa said.

"So, Lisa, are you afraid to die?"

"Yep, I am. Afraid I won't go to a nice place."

Elwood laughed. "Who did you murder?"

"No one."

"Then, not to worry. You will go to a nice place."

Lisa snickered. "Is murder all anyone goes to hell for?"

"No, but in your case, it's the only possible transgression."

Lisa looked away with a partial smile on her lips.

"Silvia, you need to look at your fear of death. Do it tonight. Then let me know what you come up with."

Elwood was matter-of-fact about such a deep fear, as if it could be conquered overnight. Yet Silvia felt peaceful and relaxed; whatever he suggested was worth a try.

The detectives officially closed the investigation after both Leo and his partner were put back in prison. But John still believed someone who wanted to stop the petition drive was behind the hit. "Leo was suggestible, easy to manipulate. Someone could have influenced him to seek revenge against me."

"Maybe, but what does it matter?" Lisa asked. "If the goal was to put a wrench in the petition drive, it didn't work."

"It's had the opposite effect," Silvia agreed. "Leo made us tougher. Before we were like feral cats." She growled and clawed the air. "Now we're tigers."

It was high noon on deadline day. John, Brad, Lisa, George and Silvia gathered around a huge copy machine at a supporting law firm to finalize their legal case. A heaviness, like gray storm clouds, hovered over them as hundreds of pages of evidentiary documents were copied and assembled. As the clock sped toward the four o'clock zero hour, they nervously waited for the phone call from the statistics guys to name the 'winner'; the TV station the petition would target. The delay was because two stations were equally biased against blacks so the data had to be tweaked to break the tie. As if one last-minute missing detail wasn't hair-raising enough, they had to wait for two of the signed and notarized affidavits from D.C.'s black leaders.

At two thirty the phone rang. John grabbed the receiver. He listened no longer than a few seconds, and then grinned from ear to ear.

"We've got the chosen one!"

George rushed to a typist to have the station's name inserted into the spaces left in his legal brief. Twenty copies of the full petition, which included two hundred pages of backup evidence, needed to reach the FCC headquarters by four o'clock. The FCC's building was a minimum twenty-minute drive away, but that time could be doubled in D.C. as rush-hour type jams were constant no matter what time of day.

Lisa and Silvia had twenty copies of the evidence rubber-banded and stacked carefully on a large table next to the copier. The office manager of the host law firm arrived and handed Silvia the two missing affidavits. She sighed and relaxed a little. They had plenty of time.

But her diminishing tension lasted only a few seconds. "Sorry, ladies, but I'll have to bump your project to make copies for our senior partner," said the office manager.

Silvia gasped and stepped in front of the woman. "No. Please no. We've got a four o'clock deadline at the FCC. Can't it wait? We need just thirty minutes more." Her voice quivered.

"Sorry, that's the way it is in the legal business, one urgent deadline after another. Now, move aside and let me get this done."

The office manager – a stocky woman with a military-type posture – glared at Silvia and spat out her words. She pushed their boxes out of her way. Lisa started to argue, but Silvia nudged her to let it go; they couldn't win and anything they said would risk a slowdown of the woman's work. Silvia looked at the men. They also sensed the office manager's tenacity and didn't interfere.

At three o'clock, they got back the use of the copier and resumed their work. John and Brad began to pick up the pages as they came out of the machine.

"Don't do that!" Lisa yelled.

Silvia's voice was loud and firm. "Stop, stop! You'll mess up the order if you pull them out now. The machine collates automatically." She had to gain control or the deadline would be lost. "If you want to get this petition in on time, you will do as I say."

Silvia paused to make eye contact and ensure she had their attention. "John and George, you go to the table. As soon as one set is complete, we'll hand it to you. Put the legal brief on top of the papers already stacked there. Insert the affidavits where you see yellow tabs. Put two rubber bands around each entire package and put the completed petition into the box. Brad, you go get the car and wait out front ready to get this box to the FCC on time – whatever it takes."

The men gawked at her wide-eyed. Usually they gave the orders for her to take. Yet by God's great and eternal grace, they complied.

At exactly 4 p.m. on September 2, 1969, the first petition-to-deny license renewal of a Washington, D.C. TV station was time stamped *RECEIVED* by the FCC. The nationwide legal war against black exclusion by the America's television stations had begun.

Most were jubilant when they gathered for a celebration at Unity House. But not Brad; he had bad news. "The reason the broadcast industry did not go all out to sabotage the petition drive was because they came up with a better idea. They sent their lobbyists over to Congress and with the speed of lightening, got a bill drafted that makes it illegal for citizens to participate in the license renewal process. It's blatant racism." Brad ran his hands through his already disheveled hair. "John, we have to testify against this. The hearings are in two days."

John banged his fist on the wall. "Jesus Christ, no time to breathe. Those MFs . . . ironic, isn't it? Big business just loves capitalism – free and open competition – as long as they are on top. But man, when anything threatens their investments, they scurry like rats to big daddy government to protect them."

Everyone went silent.

Silvia's reaction was delayed. When it came, her anger was filled with determination. "There is no way this legislation will get passed or even get out of committee. Brad, what do you need us to do?"

"First thought, we have to let them know it's racist. Our testimony should be delivered by you, John, as the director of Unity House and co-chairman of B.E.S.T. What we say will have real clout since it comes from the black community. And we've got to get the radio, TV, and newspaper reporters to cover these hearings. John, now's the time to call Ralph Zeigler; let him know we plan to raise hell."

Silvia was the only one in the front office when Elwood arrived. The others were in the conference room with what was supposed to be a beer and pizza celebration dinner. She started to walk him back but he stopped her and spoke quietly. Privately. "Could you come to my house at lunch time tomorrow? My wife will feed you, and I'll give you some inner peace." He wore his usual suit and tie but carried the fedora that he removed when he entered, like the gentleman he was.

"Yes, of course I'll be there." Elwood was spiritually advanced, Silvia was honored. Who wouldn't want inner peace? But on the other hand, after the hectic last few weeks, she was a physical wreck. What if she was a disappointment? Those thoughts passed through her mind as they walked down the hall to join the others. Elwood stopped and turned to her. "Don't worry. I know you're a physical wreck. That's why you got the invitation."

Whoa. She scrunched her forehead in an attempt to fathom what just happened. He definitely read her mind that time.

Without any fanfare, as if he'd been with the group all day, Elwood announced he had something for them to hear. He took a tape recorder out of his pocket and placed it on the table. "I had my trusty spy mechanism planted again, this time in the office of the 'Chosen One's' station manager. Thought we'd all enjoy his reaction. His visitor was that same corporate attorney you heard on that taped meeting." Elwood pushed the play button. "You'll hear the manager's voice first."

Manager: "Damn. Damn it to hell. So goddamn it, we're the chosen ones."

Attorney: "You are. They got it in just in time."

Manager: "It's not like we didn't know it was coming."

Attorney: "Well, we didn't even try to stop them. That was your call. I still think we could have turned the white woman. It's ironic that it was you that blew the whistle on the attempt."

Manager: "It was the FBI report; they labeled her a tough broad. Threatening her was too big a risk."

Attorney: "Let's go get a drink."

Manager: "Not now. Get me copies of this for my people. We have to respond; do it quick before the FCC even thinks about hearings. It's the damn time and money that's a killer." Silence lasted a few moments. "Of course, you lawyers are the ones that will reap the benefits in billed time."

Attorney: "If it makes you feel better, you won't be the only one hit with this. My contacts say many more petitions will be filed by black groups all over the country. So the FCC won't set a precedent and deny any station's license for black exclusion. B.E.S.T., of course, will appeal whatever the ruling is. It could take years – "

Manager: "But these black groups didn't do this to get our license. They want some clout to negotiate and this will give them exactly that. We will have to increase black employment, programming – whatever it takes – or the FCC will give us quotas. Much as I hate it, I know we've got to do it."

When the tape ended, everyone was silent.

"Okay, that was then. What about tomorrow or the next day if this legislation gets out of committee? We can't even relax and enjoy the fact that we got the exact reaction we wanted." John voiced what was going through Silvia's mind and from the glum looks around the table, he spoke for everyone.

At Elwood's modest home, Silvia munched his wife's delicious chicken salad and sipped a cool glass of homemade lemonade. He asked about her fear-of-death. She told him she believed death was a good thing; a great adventure that she hoped would not come any time soon.

After lunch, Elwood lit a marijuana cigarette and handed it to Silvia without comment. She eagerly inhaled and soon the aches and pains from her overheated, stressed-out body vanished. Her mood followed. Joy.

"I didn't know gurus would support smoking anything." Her voice came out soft and smooth; even her larynx was relaxed.

"You notice I'm not smoking. I'm relaxed all the time, a natural God-given high. But for you right now, it's medicinal. I don't prescribe marijuana as a substitute for meditation."

That was the end of any conversation. For the rest of the hour, Silvia's attention floated with the smooth music wafting from the stereo. She wondered if the smile on her face matched the one that was always on Elwood's. "I want to have this joy all the time, Elwood. How do I get it without smoking a joint?"

"You're almost ready to receive it."

"Receive what?"

"You'll know what when it comes."

Anyone else who was so secretive would infuriate her. But not Elwood. His spiritual level was obviously far above her's. Yet she badly wanted whatever it was.

Back to normal and back to work, Silvia was assigned to help defeat the Senate bill trying to derail their nationwide petition drive. To guide the legal issues, George sent attorney Charlie Jordan to partner with her. The first task for the twosome was to draft John's testimony – due the next day – for the Senate sub-committee hearings on Capitol Hill.

Charlie was born in America from a Chinese father and Nigerian mother, which, from Silvia's perspective, culminated into a tall, handsome, warm and intelligent human being. It didn't take long for the two to know they liked each other a lot. They were the same age, both on the verge of divorce with three children living with soon to be ex-spouses, and they shared a life mission.

Charlie outlined a strategy designed to shock the committee members with evidence of their racism. The goal was to kill the bill before it could get out of committee.

The two sat across from each other at the conference table with a stack of yellow pads and ball point pens. By happy chance, since time was of the essence, Charlie shared Silvia's team-writing notion: they would stimulate each other's creativity best if they stayed loose and playful. They kept up a steady banter, made fun of each other's word choices and used rock, paper, scissors to determine a winning phrase. They ate cold pizza and drank endless cups of hot coffee. It was after midnight when they finished the draft.

John had gone home but asked them to bring their draft to him no matter what the hour. They watched his face as he read and smiled at each other when his eyes lit up.

"This is good. Very good! I love the opening: *S.2004 is an insult to the intelligence of the American people.*"

Charlie suggested he read the whole testimony out loud – as many times as necessary – until he felt comfortable. "You need to prepare for any questions, but keep in mind that I'll sit beside you at the witness table so you can defer to me for anything."

Silvia had never seen John so nervous. She knew he had little public speaking experience – maybe none. God, if she had to speak in front of U.S. Senators as a maiden public-speaking event, she'd be terrified. She doubted John would be able to sleep the few hours he had left before it was time to go.

The next day Silvia arrived at the Capitol early to have time to enjoy the crisp autumn day. The bright sun dazzled the red-orange maple leaves into shiny blasts of color against the green of the pines. Her heart soared when she gazed at the white-domed building flanked by its hundreds of columns decorated with American flags. This country had plenty of imperfections, but nobility was steeped in the bloodless battles fought in this building to try to bring liberty and justice to all. Nobody promised democracy wouldn't be messy.

She cut across the lawns, weaving around the Keep Off the Grass signs to reach the Russell Senate Office Building where the hearings were held. Despite her three-inch heels, she walked on the earth. It felt good to sink into dirt rather than concrete sidewalks. She caught the scent of pine mixed with cut grass – food for the soul. No matter that she'd been here often, these hallowed grounds always gave her the impression that a divine presence lingered about.

She felt confident about her appearance in her chic navy-blue suit with red and white striped blouse. Her heels clicked on the marble floor as she made her way down the long corridor to the security entrance. After checking inside her purse, the guard kindly pointed the way to Hearing Room 108.

John and Charlie were already there, seated a few rows from the witness table. She moved in beside Charlie. He smiled at her and whispered, "You look nice." He put his hand on his chest and looked down to bring attention to his own outfit. He was dressed in a navy-blue suit with a red-and-white striped tie. She felt herself flush at what looked like a couple's pre-set dress code, which it wasn't. Just a coincidence.

She glanced at John. His eyes were bright, but the black circles underneath revealed his sleeplessness. He needed comfort.

"You look great, John! Especially the silk neck scarf. Nice. Like a famous film director."

He laughed nervously. "The white boys will still see me as a black militant. But then, they're right. I am on the warpath." He handed her a schedule of speakers. "Look at the list of witnesses."

John was number seven. Numbers one through six were all broadcasters, according to their listed affiliations.

The room began to fill up. Silvia was surprised to see black men and women filing in. She recognized some from Ashton's group. And there was Jackie. And Ashton. Whoa! With their own *alleluia chorus* in the audience, these hearings could turn into something great. Jubilant, she whispered to John, "Who got in touch with everyone on such short notice?"

He whispered back, "While you two had a writing party yesterday, Brad, George and I hit the phones. Looks like everyone showed up."

The bill's sponsor and committee chair, Senator Jacob Rogers, pounded the gavel to open the hearings. The first speaker owned several radio and TV stations. He pointed out the need for financial stability in an industry that required a huge capital outlay for technical equipment. For the next fifteen minutes, he detailed the expenses of running a broadcast station. Charlie nudged Silvia and pointed to the notes he was writing. *What about the lucrative income from commercials?*

All the industry witnesses stressed the urgent need to eliminate their insecurity by removing the threat of a lost license. All but one of the committee members had professed their support for the bill even before the hearings. No one questioned the fact that since the FCC began thirty years ago, only a handful of licenses had ever been revoked. No one asked how the bill would impact the airwave owners – the viewing public.

Then the game changed. It began with John's description of how the bill would take away the citizens' rights to a responsive television industry. "It would give broadcasters their licenses in perpetuity." He accused Senator Rogers of writing a bill that would forever bar blacks from the industry. "This is a racist bill."

The Senator's face grew red, and he waved a finger in the air. "If there's one thing I don't want you people to go away with, it's the idea that this is a racist bill!"

"It is! It is!" shouted the chorus of visitors.

Most in the hearing room knew that dozens more petitions-to-deny license renewals would be filed within weeks. The timing for this legislation was triggered to keep the pesky citizen groups at bay.

Senator Rogers looked like he was about to burst into tears so John tried to put him at ease. "We're not calling *you* a racist, Senator. It's your bill."

Another opposition speaker made fun of a broadcaster who testified that the bill was necessary 'to remove a Sword of Damocles that hung by a thin hair over their heads', causing them to tremble with fear for their licenses. "Our experience shows that if there is such a sword, it rests securely in the hands of the FCC, which grimly uses it to fight off members of the public who seek justice as rightful owners of the airwaves."

Uproarious laughter came from the crowd. At that, one of the FCC commissioners stormed out of the room, his face bright red. Senator Rogers sighed deeply. "I've never seen a bill so maligned," he said, and gaveled the meeting to a close.

As the Unity House team walked back to the office, Charlie and Silvia skipped and swung their arms like happy children. Two Senators on the committee had already withdrawn their support. The bill would surely die of natural causes.

Suddenly Charlie stopped and put his arm out to halt Silvia. "How would you like to go to dinner with me tonight?"

A formal date? It was a scary thought. What about the kids? On the other hand, Charlie was such a good guy. "Yes, of course. I'd love it!"

Charlie chose the perfect ambience for their night out – Blues Alley in Georgetown with Ramsey Lewis playing the piano. The tones from the maestro's magical fingers soothed her nerves; like every cell was being massaged. She was high, mostly from the music, when Charlie walked her to the front door.

"This was a beautiful night, Charlie. The music, the food, the company."

He pulled her into his arms. Their lingering kiss was passionate and tender. For a moment they looked deep into each other's eyes. Then they kissed again.

Long after Charlie had gone, she touched a finger to her mouth and felt his warmth.

5

It was the weekend with the kids and a beautiful Indian summer day – perfect weather for a canoe trip to Roosevelt Island. Silvia chose to cross the Potomac opposite Thompson's Boat House where the currents were fast enough to give the kids a challenge that would bolster self-confidence. At an early age they learned to swim and handle boats; they knew how to keep balance in a canoe.

As they neared the shore, Silvia reminded Frankie about his job. "When we touch land, you remember the drill? You step out first and hold the boat steady so the rest of us can get out without tipping over."

"I got it," Frankie said, his nose in the air.

Silvia hid her smile. His haughtiness came from his ego, inflated with pride as front paddler. He had successfully supplied the right amount of power to keep the canoe steady across the swift currents.

When the boat glanced the shore, Frankie stepped out, pulled the canoe parallel to land and held it in place. But as Alan stood to move forward, Frankie grinned, and rocked the boat.

"You rat!" Alan shouted as he lunged in a desperate attempt to shift weight and regain balance. But too late. The canoe tipped and dumped Alan, Linda, Silvia and the picnic lunch into the blue-green algae that clogged the shallow waters next to the shore.

For a moment, no one moved. Then Silvia, with weeds clinging to her soaked head, waded over to a laughing Frankie who stood – dry – on the shore. She laughed too as she pulled him into the river. The inevitable splash battle ensued while they watched their peanut butter and jelly sandwiches float away.

The spill turned out to be a happy event for Silvia as it led to a rare quiet moment with her kids lying beside her as they dried in the warmth of the sun. They marveled at the brilliant blue sky and quibbled over the animal shapes in the cloud formations. Then Frankie got serious.

"Mom, when are you coming back? I don't like being at Grandma's; she doesn't let us go anywhere. I can't even ride my bike to my friend's house on the next block."

"Yeah," Linda agreed. "And she says bad things about you."

"Really?" Silvia gritted her teeth to stop herself from instinctively lashing out. She looked up at the sky to elevate her response.

"No matter what she says about me, she loves you so much. She worries that you'll get hurt or lost if she can't see you on the street. She's old, you know. You all need to be kind to her."

"Even if she's mean?" Alan asked. "Sometimes she tells me to shut my mouth."

"Yeah, Alan argues with her all the time," Linda said.

"Do you talk to Dad about all of this? What does he say?"

"You know Dad," Linda said. "He just listens, gives us a hug and doesn't say anything."

"I'll talk to him. At least about letting you go to your friend's, Frankie." God, what to tell them about coming back. Frank wouldn't even look at her.

"I still haven't finished the work I'm doing, but I need you three to keep being happy most of the time so Grandma and Dad are happy too."

She put an end to the subject. "So who's hungry? Let's take the canoe back and find the nearest McDonald's."

Cheers erupted and scared a flock of geese from their feeding ground. They squawked loudly, scolding the shouters as they flew away.

Thoughts of Charlie seeped into Silvia's attention when it should have been elsewhere. Her eyes never left the screen when she and her housemates watched

Walter Cronkite deliver the news, yet she didn't hear a word. Instead, she wondered where Charlie was at that moment or what he would think about this or that. When she caught herself distracted she felt silly; like a seventh grade girl who had a crush on some boy.

As fate would have it, a few days after their date, John put Charlie and Silvia together again on a project. The job was to map out a strategy to persuade the President of the United States to appoint a black commissioner to the FCC. Silvia was eager to help get a black perspective added to the government regulators who could ensure broadcasters reached a more diverse audience than only white suburbanites.

When Charlie stepped in the door at Unity House, he looked so handsome Silvia swallowed a gasp. He smiled at her with such obvious warmth heat rushed to her cheeks. She wasn't ready for John and Lisa, who stood beside her, to suspect something was going on.

John gave them their orders. "You two draft an outline for the campaign. That'll be the starting point you can bounce off the rest of us."

They walked back to the conference room, and to Silvia's chagrin, Charlie closed the door. Her face stayed hot but she tried to be cool. "We don't shut doors around here unless it's a private meeting."

"It's private," he said as he wrapped his arms around her and kissed her firmly.

She surrendered into the tenderness of his strong arms. He pulled back and looked into her eyes. "I thought if we got this over with, we could buckle down and put our attention on the FCC. Yes?"

Silvia's cool was blown. When she stopped laughing, she suggested he open the door "or Lisa and John will come back here and tease us to death."

He winked, opened the door and, with a flourish, set his briefcase on the table. "Now let's begin."

In a few hours they had a plan. The elements included agreements from several U.S. senators to recommend black candidates for the next available post. B.E.S.T. would identify and vet three candidates and hold multiple press conferences to introduce them. Endorsements for the concept would be gathered from all major black associations – businesses, churches, political and civil rights groups. They would seek editorials in support of a black commissioner from *The Washington Post*, the *Evening Star*, and *The Wall Street Journal*.

When John came in to check on their progress, Charlie told him the outline was ready. "But, sorry to tell you, the campaign has to begin tomorrow. Either you or Ashton need to testify at the Senate hearing to confirm President Nixon's nominations for the new commissioner. It's too late to get a black nominee in this time, but they need to hear our case now, before the next vacancy comes up."

John sat down, crossed his legs and lit up a cigarette. "God, it's a rat race to keep up with these guys. I'll see if Ashton can do it. You guys go ahead and get B.E.S.T. on the docket and then draft up something for him to say."

At the confirmation hearings, John, Brad, Lisa, Charlie and Silvia sat together in the front row. The candidates – both white males – were being gently interviewed and praised frequently by the senators, even though one candidate had been chairman of the Republican National Committee and the other a broadcast station manager. Apparently, the government's criteria that commissioners be politically neutral and void of industry connections didn't apply to these two. The interviews ended with all the senators expressing their support.

Then, abruptly, when Ashton strolled to the witness table looking relaxed and confident, the mood changed. His afro was bushy, his shirt was a brightly colored African dashiki and he carried a copy of Eldridge Cleaver's *Soul on Ice*. The Unity House group hid their smiles – the costume was Ashton's own touch. Silvia studied the senators. They became quiet and sat rigidly in their chairs. Their once-friendly expressions now looked apprehensive. Silvia wondered if Ashton would stay on script.

In a clear, firm voice he began on the course they had charted. He scolded the broadcast industry for its exclusion of black Americans, sometimes quoting the Kerner Commission report and often referencing the 1934 Communications Act. He laid out the statistical evidence proving nearly zero black presence in the industry. When he reported on the results of his research into the civil rights records of the two candidates, there were audible gasps from some senators.

"We challenge you to find one – just one – instance whereby either of these candidates have said or done anything in their entire lives to support racial equality."

Then he went off script.

"Under these commissioners, the FCC will become more racist, more antithetical to black progress and more opposed to integrated programming. Black people have different dreams, different hopes, different aspirations, different lifestyles. Yet those are never seen on TV. Instead, the programming to date depicts blacks like twentieth-century minstrels – they sing, they dance, they shuffle and carry the water pail for golf pros."

A hush fell over the chamber. Finally, the chairman asked if either of the candidates wanted to respond. Silvia was astonished that the chairman would expect them to give an off-the-cuff response to being called a racist. But one candidate, his face red and his voice laced with anger, did speak. He said he was not a racist and never had been. Then he paused; his voice mellowed. "Unfortunately, I've never known any black person well. I have no friends who are black."

Silvia was taken aback. He was declaring a human desire for friendship. His naked honesty touched her heart. Maybe there is hope for the future?

As they continued to work close together on issues that reflected their shared values, Charlie and Silvia's personal relationship deepened. At first she was cautious; uneasy about how the children would react. Then one evening on the phone, Linda told her Frank had brought a blonde-haired lady named Kate home for dinner.

"They went out to a movie by themselves – without us." Linda's concern was more about the missed movie than for her father's interest in another woman. If he could date, and do it without the kids getting upset, so could she. Silvia saw the orange light turn green and jumped into a passionate love affair with Charlie.

After work they played together at D.C.'s endless feast of restaurants and music clubs. Their social compatibility was the same as their workplace rapport – harmonious.

Silvia's housemates knew Charlie only from the brief moments when he came to pick her up. But now that she was so often away from the house with him, they complained. They missed her and wanted to get to know Charlie better. Silvia agreed to cook dinner for everyone on a weeknight when they could all be there.

Silvia loved dinner parties. Not only did they provide a chance to please the guests in their solar-plexus, but table conversations in pleasant surroundings often revealed the diners deeper selves. The menu was simple: chicken tetrazzini that she could prepare before going to work, a tossed green salad and garlic bread. Dessert required no cooking – vanilla ice cream with dark chocolate syrup and whipped cream. Her favorite. She got up at 5 a.m. on dinner day to get the main dish ready to put in the oven when she got home.

Silvia and Charlie were in the kitchen preparing dinner when the first housemate to arrive home joined them in the kitchen. Dakotah Penman was a lawyer and Lakota tribe member whose permanent residence was on a reservation where he lived with his wife and two college age children. He had come to D.C. several months ago to waken the president and congress to the brutality of tribal conditions.

Charlie handed him a beer.

"How goes it?" Dakotah asked.

"Real good." Charlie hoisted his beer bottle to toast. "To us lawyers who fight for a cause, poor and overworked."

Dakotah laughed and clinked his beer with Charlie's. "You've got that right. That's the problem with having a conscience. Silvia tells me you're with them on the TV stuff."

"Yep, I like what I do. How about you?"

"I can't say I like it but it's necessary for our survival. We're negotiating with Nixon to get us out from under the termination policies."

Charlie jerked his head up. "Termination? What in hell are those?"

"Genocide," Dakotah said. "In the 1940's the government wanted us to become like them. You know, civilized. But it didn't take. So they got fed up. Broke all the treaties, took away our sovereignty, took away our children, tried to force us to get jobs in the cities, wear suits, worship only Jesus and pay taxes." His face showed no emotion. Then he smiled. "Nice guys, huh?"

Silvia chopped the vegetables faster. She had heard it before, but each hearing increased her outrage.

For Charlie, it was news. "Damn, brother." He shook his head in disgust. "So what's happening now?"

"Believe it or not, President Nixon doesn't like the termination policies either. Neither did LBJ, but he didn't do anything about it. Nixon's taken our advice and promised to issue a policy statement that ends it. But it's not a done deal until we get it through congress. Money's involved, so you know it's a big push. Of course, we won't get anywhere close to what we need but it's better than being terminated." He pulled his finger across his throat to mimic a slicing knife, and chuckled.

Dakotah told more about the terrible conditions suffered by his people, including the blatant racism. He cocked his head and with a sly smile said, "That's why I push Silvia to come over to our side – help conquer the worst of American stupidity."

Silvia never took Dakotah's come-and-work-with-us requests seriously, so had not mentioned it to anyone. Charlie gave her a quizzical look, with raised eyebrows and a tight mouth.

To keep up his mischief, Dakotah said, "Hey, brother, are you jealous?"

"Na," Charlie said and winked at Silvia. "Just not ready to let go of a good worker."

The rest of the housemates piled into the kitchen. Beer and banter flowed nonstop until Silvia had to concentrate and banished them to the living room. Several times Carol or Dakotah came in and asked if they had missed the bell. Each time Silvia laughed and shooed them out.

Silvia finally rang the triangle bell announcing dinner was ready. The clanging reverberations were more traditional of a Western cowboy ranch than a fancy Eastern mansion. Carol had established the bell call system because the house was too large for the people on the third floor to hear a shout. It was a household joke for the hungry mob to take turns wandering into the kitchen to harass the cook with 'Did it ring? Did I miss it?'

When all were seated and the tasting begun, Marilyn spoke. "Silvia, I'm surprised. This is delicious! Quite an improvement over the hamburgers and hotdogs you usually give us when the kids are here. Charlie, you must truly be special; we had no clue she could cook." Marilyn was an environmental lawyer, but in her spare time she cooked like a gourmet chef. No one missed dinner when it was her turn.

Charlie grinned. Silvia grunted. "I'll take that as a compliment, Marilyn dear, but it's not nice to be sarcastic."

"Great news!" said Tom, who was an anti-Vietnam War stalwart. "Today, along with a few others in our group, we met face-to-face with our archenemy, Henry Kissinger." He looked triumphant, giddy with excitement.

"Ah, a slick one is that guy," said Carol, who didn't trust anyone in the current government. "Nixon's buddy."

"Yeah, we all had him pegged as the demon that kept the war going. But no, he hates the war. Said it could never be won. Can you believe it? We were stunned!" Tom sipped his wine, then gestured with his glass. "He took the time to talk with each one of us separately. Wanted to know the details of our protests. Told us everyone in the administration didn't agree with him yet, but he would keep at it. By the time we left, we were convinced he didn't have horns."

Silvia was stunned; she took a sip of wine. Then she took another. "That's the second good thing I've heard today about the Nixon administration. What's going on? God forbid – what if our enemy becomes our friend? Who among us could live without a bad guy to fight?"

Silvia raised her hand. Carol raised her's and then Tom. But Marilyn and the other guys shook their heads. "Nope, we're lawyers," Charlie said. "We have to make a living."

Silvia was glad for the house rule that the cook did not do the clean-up. With her mates on duty in the kitchen, she and Charlie had the living room to themselves. They relaxed on the couch.

"These are good people you live with," Charlie said. "Everyone working on a different cause. And you didn't know each other before?"

"Carol and I knew each other. It does seem weird that we came together like this. The group is fascinating. And intriguing people come to visit. There's this guy – calls himself Scrappy – who's a friend of John's. He says he's retired black Mafia. About fifty years old. Came up from the South when he was young without even a clean shirt. Lived in stark poverty until some Mafia chief gave him a way to make a living."

"No such thing as retired Mafia. Are you sure he's okay to have around?"

"He's small and thin, doesn't look like Mafia. We let him come because he's studying us. Says he can't believe anybody would work for nothing just because they believe in some cause. He tries to poke holes in what we say, find our *real* motive. Ironically, there's usually a U.S. attorney here at the same time – Marilyn's boyfriend. He's an interesting case too. He knows we all smoke pot, when we have it. But he asks us not to smoke it when he's around. He said he wouldn't arrest us, but he doesn't want to be a hypocrite."

They chuckled about the odd mix of friends. Silvia relished the insight into radically different life styles without having to live them.

She should have paid attention to Charlie's warning. On her way to Unity House one morning, Scrappy pulled up beside her in his old Cadillac and offered a lift to work. She didn't hesitate since it was only a few blocks. As they got closer, he asked her to take a quick look at a house he was planning to buy nearby.

He unlocked the front door and ushered Silvia in. The window shades were all pulled down, so the room was too dark to inspect. As she moved to let in the light, Scrappy grabbed her shoulders.

"What the hell are you doing?"

"We're having sex, that's what's doing." His tone was threatening.

"What?" At first she though he must be kidding. When she saw his solemn face and stance, firmly planted to fight, she growled at him. "No way in hell." She jerked out of his hold and moved quickly toward the door. With an iron grip, he caught her arm, reached to a table and snatched up a knife. He held the knife to her throat and pushed her against the wall.

Furiously, with every ounce of strength she could muster, she shoved her foot into his stomach. He flew backwards, almost falling, but regained balance. He lunged toward her, pointing the blade. She kicked again, her long legs aiming for his private parts. But he side-stepped the blow, threw down his knife and grabbed her with both arms so tightly she couldn't move. Her heart raced; she gasped for breath.

"Stop!" she said. "Give me some time." She needed to think. He pulled her over to a chair and pushed her in. He stood beside her, knife in hand, breathing heavily.

It took her a minute to realize she wasn't going to win a physical fight. He had a weapon, and steely strength. No one would come to her rescue because no one knew where she was. This wasn't worth dying over.

"You know that sex with me won't give you whatever it is you're looking for; you'll get the opposite. This will end our friendship . . . your relationship with everyone at the house is finished. Also with John. You'll get nothing."

"I know what I want, and I always get what I want. By force, if necessary." His voice was harsh, his face menacing. He waved his knife. He was Mafia.

"Let's get it over with."

He pulled her to the next room, where a bed had been set up. Good God, he'd planned the whole thing! He kept the knife in his hand as he arranged himself and her for the rape.

Eyes closed, cold and trembling, she waited and waited. Finally she knew the truth. Her eyes flew open.

He was impotent.

He began to whimper like a child. He wouldn't be raping anyone. The knife dropped to the floor.

She slid out from under him and fixed her clothes, still trembling. As she backed toward the door, he sat up and wiped his eyes with the back of his hand. In a feeble voice filled with tears, he said he thought for certain she would be the one that could bring him back to normal.

Now more furious than afraid and her voice thick with wrath, she shouted, "Don't think about coming near the house again – ever! The friendship is over. You go to hell!"

She stormed out and ran until she calmed down. What should she do? Go to the police? Call Charlie? She decided it would be too messy if the police got involved. A court case that charged rape by a Mafia member, one that she had befriended, not only made her charges weak but wasn't worth the risk of retaliation by his buddies. And to call Charlie seemed like a bad idea. Not that she cared if Scrappy got beat up, but Charlie could get hurt. Still, she had to talk to somebody.

Elwood.

She was relieved to find him at home. When she finished her story, for a moment she felt okay. But as soon as she relaxed, memories of the knife and Scrappy's hands all over her, whirled through her head.

"Silvia?" Elwood patted her arm. He asked her to close her eyes and sit in silence. It took a few minutes for the inner screams to subside, but soon she felt his soothing energy. Twenty minutes later, her hot head had cooled. Elwood asked if she recognized anything good out of the event.

"Good? Maybe that I won't be so naïve again. Geez, trusting Mafia types." She sighed. "How stupid."

Elwood smiled. "Anything else?"

Sylvia pondered but found nothing.

93

"Never mind," Elwood said. "I'll walk you to Unity House. They are wondering where you are."

That night when she told Charlie, he held her close until she convinced him that she was okay; still angry but the trauma had faded. He paced around the apartment like a bull. "I could have him locked up for life. It would be easy to get a conviction except for the Mafia complication. They tend to shoot anyone who testifies against one of their own."

"It feels like a diversion of our precious time and energy to bother with such a loser as Scrappy." Silvia said. "He's not worth any decent person having to go into witness protection or being murdered. Our priority is fighting racism."

Charlie agreed but said he would like to be the one to tell John about the attempted rape. "He may have more creative, less legal ways of dealing with Scrappy. Ways we wouldn't want to know about."

Sure enough, when John heard about Scrappy's obscene violation of Silvia, he said he would take care of it. "And you'll never have to lay eyes on Scrappy again."

When Silvia's housemates heard about it, being warriors for justice, they had an immediate desire to see Scrappy thrown in jail for life. But they too backed down when told about the dangers, time and energy required to make that happen. "When your mission is to fix a particular injustice, the negative forces will try to grab your attention away," Silvia said. "Zero of my attention is going to that scum bag."

She kept wondering about Elwood's query. What was the something more she could have learned from the incident? After many recitals of the story, it dawned upon her. Two times – twice – she'd escaped from an actual rape. She bowed her head; her heart swelled. She gave silent gratitude to whatever or whoever was the invisible force protecting her.

6

One month later, Winter came to cool down the citizens of D.C. Their day's work done, Charlie and Silvia were at their favorite bar, snuggled into a booth while they gazed into a blazing fire. The Hawk 'n' Dove was within walking distance of the Capitol and touted itself as the perfect haven for politicians, on both sides of the isle, to work out any differences over food, drink and geniality.

"I have to take a week off next month for my niece's wedding, remember?" Silvia asked.

Charlie nodded.

"Denver's nice. Wanna come with me?"

Charlie grimaced.

She laughed and put her head against his shoulder. "You don't want to meet my whole family?"

"It doesn't feel like the right time. Does it to you?"

She picked up her head. They never talked about their relationship. Truth was, she would never be intimate with a guy she didn't want to marry. But no way would she say that to him. "You're right; it's not the time." She quickly changed the subject. "Shall we eat dinner at your place? We can pick up some shrimp. I'll make scampi."

A tinge of fear gripped her chest.

Silvia, whose college major was journalism, had high regard for the profession. She was thrilled when John asked her to try to get *The Washington Post* to take an editorial position in favor of a black FCC commissioner. She telephoned for an appointment with a revered editorial page editor who she targeted because his opinions reflected hers, especially about racism. To her surprise, he answered the phone in person and agreed to meet.

The editor's desk was in the middle of a bullpen crowded with busy reporters. She was awed by their ability to concentrate despite the cacophony of voices, typewriters and presses. When he beckoned her to a seat beside his desk she grinned, unable to hide her school-girl excitement to be amongst this famous editor and some of the best news reporters in the country.

Silvia immediately got to the point. "The riots and their after effects created an urgent need to add the perspective of a black person to the FCC." She went on with her spiel to point out how an editorial from such a prominent newspaper would give a powerful boost to the idea. Before she could finish, he interrupted.

"You don't have to convince me. There's no question we need a black FCC commissioner, and yes, I will write an editorial that says so. I'll do it right away. Your timing is good. Nixon can start to consider candidates well before the next vacancy."

"You'll write the editorial yourself?" He nodded. "Wonderful!" Silvia stood and extended her hand "Thank you, thank you." She hoped he couldn't hear her thumping heart.

He held her hand in his for a moment. "Is your group making recommendations?"

"Uh . . . yes. We're vetting candidates; we have too many now. We're at the narrowing-down stage."

"That's good. Okay. I'll write the editorial soon. And, Silvia, I appreciate you bringing this to my attention."

Her heart soared. Although her feet never left the sidewalk, she flew back to Unity House.

Before she left town for the wedding, Silvia used some leave time to catch up on long neglected medical check-ups. She splurged on a new dress and matching shoes.

The wedding played out like a *Bridal Magazine* story. The day was gloriously sunny. Rays of light blazed through the kaleidoscopic windows to signal that God was watching, so said the comedic preacher who performed the ceremony. The elegant reception, held at a nearby inn, included a sit-down dinner, plenty of booze, and dancing to a live orchestra.

Silvia sat with two elder aunts as they watched her senior citizen parents dominate the dance floor with their smooth moves. According to the aunts, the couple's perfectly synchronized maneuvers could only happen if their relationship was in excellent harmony. Silvia, who drank more wine than usual, bluntly told her aunts their analysis was wrong.

"Frank and I were always in perfect harmony on the dance floor, but we don't live in perfect harmony. In fact, we're getting a divorce."

Both aunts looked surprised; it was news to them. They offered sympathy but told her not to worry. Their harmony-dance theory was iron clad and meant she and Frank would get back together some day.

Silvia looked at them with raised eyebrows and scoffed. "Not possible. Not in this lifetime."

When her parents returned to the table, Silvia asked her mother to join her on a trip to the ladies' room. They hooked arms and began to walk.

"I need to tell you something personal."

"What, dear?" Her mother stopped and turned to look at her.

"I got some bad pap smear results. Just before I left my doctor called. He gave me an appointment for the day after I get home so he can give me the details face-to-face. I'm telling you now because I need someone to lean on."

"Have you had symptoms? Like heavy bleeding?"

"Yes, but thought it was work stress and would go away."

"Are you planning to tell the kids?"

"Not unless there's something to tell, and I hope there won't be. Please just give me your good thoughts. That's the kind of support I'll need for a while."

"You've got my positive attention, darling. Make sure you keep me up-to-date. I would hate to give you more than you need."

Silvia laughed, grateful her mother had the good sense and the ability to elevate her perspective away from worry when she sensed someone else's fear needed to be deflated.

The day after she returned from Denver, Silvia met with her gynecologist.

"At your age, you should have everything taken out," the doctor said. "A radical hysterectomy. We should schedule the surgery as soon as possible."

Before he moved his practice to D.C., the doctor was a senior gynecologist at one of the most advanced cancer research and treatment facilities in New York City.

"I'd like to know exactly where it is, and tell me, what is cancer anyway?" His treatment sounded extreme to her.

"I won't get into that level of detail about the pathology with you."

"Why not?"

"It would only put more fear into you. I can describe the surgery in detail."

"Well, uh, uh . . . I need to know more about what I'm dealing w – "

"You don't need to deal with it. We'll take care of everything."

That did it! Silvia stood and held her hand out to the doctor. "Thanks for the diagnosis. But you understand that I need another opinion on this."

The doctor looked startled as he limply shook her hand.

That evening, Silvia and Charlie were settled on the couch after dinner. "Charlie, I need to tell you something." He didn't look up from his newspaper but Silvia continued, her voice quivered. "I got a negative report from a test I had just before I went to the wedding. It says I may have cervical cancer."

"What?" Charlie put the paper down; his face stiffened. "You say *may* have. What do you know?" He wrapped his arms around her. He looked alarmed.

To ease his fear – and hers – she wanted to be brave. "Hey, don't fall for that 'cancer monster' stuff. I'm sure it's not very far along. I believe fear is what kills, so I'm not having any of it."

Charlie's eyebrows lifted. "Really, not afraid? How can you not be?"

"Well, what's the worst that can happen?"

"Death. Some people die of cancer, Silvia." His voice was almost a whisper.

"Well, I have no intention of dying from something as mundane as cancer. Maybe falling off a mountain or being shot behind enemy lines, but not from some disease."

"So what now?"

She told Charlie what the doctor said. "He's more afraid of cancer than I am. No way will I allow him to treat me. I have to find a doctor who at least knows that it's the body that heals, not the doctor."

Charlie continued to be anxious. "You're not one of those types that's going to use herbal tea to treat yourself?"

"No, I'm not that flaky. But I'll find a doctor who will at least try to find a more natural way to clear this up."

"Do you think that's wise?"

"I know there's something out there that heals. Or something in here." She put her hand on her heart. "What's the point of cutting out cancer cells if that doesn't get to the root of the problem? It seems to me it will just come back again."

"Okay. Find another doctor – nothing wrong with a second opinion. But do it now."

She called a friend and got the name of a doctor who had encouraged the use of alternative methods that were effective to treat some post-pregnancy problems.

The two doctors were complete opposites. The second one, whose credentials included degrees from Harvard and Johns Hopkins, assured her it was safe to take a month to try to heal herself. He had a newly designed instrument using mirrors and light that enabled her to see the inflamed area so she could pinpoint exactly where the problem was. He patiently answered all her questions and provided reading materials in case she wanted to dig deeper. She left his office exuberant, as if she was off on a great adventure. The mission was to conquer a demon that had taken up residence inside of her.

She shared her plan with Charlie, her parents, Elwood and her housemates. She would search bookstores for methods of healing that felt right. She would go on a highly nutritious diet. She would get at least eight hours of sleep every night. She would seek positive attention from relatives and friends – no worry, no fear.

Elwood was the only optimist. He agreed that her direction was a good one and that she should go with her instincts. Of course he would give her good energy.

Her other confidants were less optimistic, but since the doctor had said okay, they promised to try to give positive attention. But only for one month.

The Potter's House bookstore was Silvia's research place. They had a large selection of self-healing type books, and they sold brewed coffee. She moved among the volumes, scanned for relevance until she had a stack that seemed like they might be helpful. Over coffee, she delved in until she found the book that felt right. The author was a medical doctor with the Mayo Clinic and Johns Hopkins. He had found a way to harness what he called the "life force energy within" and used that force to heal. His first patient was himself when he healed a life threatening disease with the harnessed energy. Then he cited case studies of seriously ill patients who he guided through the same energy method and they also became healed. At the end of his clinical descriptions, he prescribed his technique. The patient should laser focus the attention "filled with unconditional love" on the diseased place for at least ten minutes twice a day.

Silvia was in seventh heaven; the treatment sounded exactly right. She could verify that to focus loving attention on a person with emotional upset, helped them come into balance. She did that with her own family members and close friends when they were troubled, so why couldn't it work on physical problems inside her own body?

She immediately put the newly found treatment to a test. Sitting cross legged in the middle of her bed – a comfortable, quiet place – she took a few deep breaths. When fully relaxed, her attention went to her children until the love she felt for them swelled her heart. Beamed on that love, she swirled her love-filled attention in a circular motion on the diseased place for the prescribed minutes. The treated area felt tingly; something was happening. At least if it didn't work, it couldn't have any damaging side effects.

Next, instead of using the telephone to enlist the support of her other family members and intimate friends, she wrote them a letter.

I need your help. I've been diagnosed with early stage cervical cancer. It's a common type and usually can be healed successfully. Surgery is the common treatment. But since cutting out the problem doesn't get to the root cause, I'd like to try some methods I've learned to see if they'll work. Then, if they don't, of course I'll have the surgery.

So what can you do? I truly believe in the power of collective positive attention. So first of all, believe it is possible this can be healed and I will be fine. Think about my situation only in a positive way. If you worry, you'll send worry to me, which could undermine the healing work. If you feel fear, you'll send that to me, which will trigger my fear, which will only help the cancer grow. So please send me your loving attention as often and as forcefully as you can. The doctor gave me a month to try my methods. Then, at the end of the month, he'll do lab tests to know whether or not we have succeeded.

I'm sending you my deepest love and appreciation for your efforts on my behalf. I know you'll probably want to talk to me on the phone about all of this, so feel free to call. I just used this method first so you would have some space to work out your reactions.

Love, Silvia

Her oldest sister, Charlotte, the analytical one, called first. She wanted to be certain that the doctor had the proper credentials. Once satisfied, she told Silvia she loved her and would suspend her doubts, but only for one month. It was pretty much the same with everyone else. They checked credentials but they also checked Silvia's disposition, whatever her words and voice could tell them. No one argued with her point that worry and fear were harmful for one's health.

To round out the laser-love treatment, she set-up a healthy routine. Every workday on her way to Unity House, she stopped at the Eastern Market to drink a six-ounce glass of fresh carrot juice. She cooked fresh vegetables and chicken or fish, with light sautéing or steam. Fresh fruit was the snack food. She went to bed early enough to ensure eight hours of sleep. Alcohol and cigarettes were banned, yet marijuana was allowed when she could get some. Charlie and her roommates were sweet and gave the space and support she needed to stick to her routine. Since it was only for one month, her discipline was pristine. She felt healthier and more vibrant than at any time in her adult life.

It was a workday and several weeks had passed since the senate confirmed Nixon's nominees for FCC commissioner. In less than a year, a term would end for another sitting commissioner, which would give Nixon an opportunity to put forth a black candidate for senate approval. John asked Silvia and Charlie to draft a letter to the president about the need for a black person to be his next nominee.

"We need to spell out for him exactly why a black perspective is needed," Charlie said.

Twenty minutes later, Silvia read him her opening graph.

"Dear President Nixon. Since the public media, especially television, profoundly influences our attitudes about people and events, we need to ensure it treats all of us fairly. Nearly 100 percent of the producers, directors, journalists, announcers and owners of television and radio stations have experienced life in America as white people; mostly men. Hence, it is understandable that such media can unknowingly distort or exaggerate their coverage about the behaviors and attitudes of blacks, women and other minorities. But such skewed perspectives can result in devastating outcomes for those who have been misunderstood. It can result in prejudice that affects hiring decisions, school admittance, housing loans, judicial decisions and treatment by police. Equally devastating, the media's distorted influence can reduce self-esteem as well as trust in American institutions by those who are being undermined."

Silvia was pleasantly surprised when Charlie said he'd use her paragraph. She was used to having her first draft mutilated when writing with others. It took years of experience as a team writer before she gained control of her ego when her 'brilliant' writing was altered or thrown out altogether.

Charlie said he'd take it from there. "Why don't you get with John and find out who he wants to recommend in this letter?"

John was on the phone when she got to his office, but he beckoned her in. She tuned in to his conversation and heard that something was a bad idea.

"Nope, no way. We'll get back to you." He hung up the phone. "That was my contact in the senate. He tossed out a name – a black candidate – as a test balloon."

"Oh yeah? Who? Sounded like you said no."

"Maybe I shouldn't tell you, of all people. No, I won't tell you. Not yet. Let me talk it over with other team members first. I'll get back to you." With a sly grin, he waved her out of his office.

An hour later, John called her back. Charlie, Lisa and Brad were already there. They looked at her with solemn faces, eyes intense. Clearly they were worried that she might not like what she was about to hear.

"The senator wanted to know if we would agree if he recommended Jataria Drucker." John's brows were raised. "What do you think about her?"

Silvia's heart swelled; a powerful woman. The senator wasn't considering some wimpy black person who wouldn't make waves. "Fantastic!"

"Now just hold on. I said no. Not her. You heard me."

Judas Priest, how could he? She felt heat flooding her face. She stammered, "Wh-why not?"

"I've talked it over with everyone. They agreed that I did the right thing. She's not the type of person we want to represent us. She's too aggressive. Too political. She can be dynamite, all right, but she doesn't compromise. Too bullheaded."

Anger seeped into Silvia's brain and she didn't try to stem it. "Oh really? Isn't it because she's a she? Can't have a black woman before a black man on the FCC." Her sarcasm forced itself out of her mouth.

"No." Charlie's voice was firm. "It's not her gender, it's her disposition. We aim to put soul in television, not anger. She alienates everyone."

Silvia cooled down since it was Charlie that made the observation. She looked at Lisa to make sure she agreed. Lisa nodded.

"Okay, okay, I get it." Silvia's voice cracked. She couldn't support Jataria if her teammates believed she would generate more heat than light.

A wave of sadness passed over her. It was difficult to be a strong woman in this man's world. And triple the difficulty if the woman was black.

When the prescribed month was over and Silvia's vitals were thoroughly tested, she met with the doctor to hear the results.

"It's amazing. I'm flabbergasted!" he said. "No trace of cancer cells anywhere. Everything's clear." He smiled at Silvia, his eyes soft and friendly; his demeanor open. "So what did you do?"

"The main treatment came from a book by a doctor with the Mayo Clinic who used it on himself first, and then on patients willing to try alternative treatments."

"So, what was the treatment?"

"It's hard to describe. He used the life force energy. It's not something that can be seen, not even when you dissect a body." She shook her head. "I'd say it's something like human electronics."

He laughed. "You can call it spiritual energy," he said. "I do."

"Are you making fun of me?"

"Not at all. I know it's the body that heals, not us doctors. I'm interested in any treatment that works."

Silvia described the treatment as well as the nutritious meals, the carrot juice, the sleep, the ban on alcohol and cigarettes. He listened carefully, but didn't ask any more questions. When the appointment ended, the doctor smiled and said he hoped not to see her again until her six-months checkup.

That night, Charlie and Silvia sat on the couch, embracing the good news. "Did you tell him about the marijuana?"

"Umm . . . No. Since it's illegal. And I'd been using it for years before I got the cancer diagnosis, so it didn't prevent it. Who knows what's the cause? Anyhow, the doctor was suddenly brusque, so didn't go any further." She was disappointed by the doctor's lack of desire to learn more about this miraculous treatment. But with the next thought, her attitude changed. "Well, you know, he would never leap into an investigation of something so radically different from his traditional medicine. At least he gave me the time and legitimized my recovery with his tests."

"So now can we go out and celebrate? You ready to have a drink?"

"Yes!" The cancer was gone. And she had proof that the love inside a person can be a colossal force.

Still a shadow loomed that she wasn't ready to share. The doctor *also* said she had to be cancer free for five years before she could be declared cured.

7

With proof that love can subdue cancer, Silvia's spiritual seeking intensified. There was much greater knowledge out there somewhere and it had to be found. Ablaze with hope, she hounded Elwood who grew exasperated with her questions and sent her away to look for herself. She scanned hundreds of books, but found them empty of anything useful. She sought out other self-professed gurus, yet found them to be fakers when they didn't feel right and required money for their wisdom.

Finally Elwood learned about a woman who he said was spiritually higher than himself. "She can give self-realization to the masses. I have never been able to do that. She's coming to town and will get you off my back." He showed her a poster with the woman's photo. Silvia's heart took a leap.

She told Charlie about it. "Her picture struck me somehow. Like familiar maybe? Or just awesome. I've gotta go hear what she has to say."

"What does she speak about?"

"Spiritual stuff. She's obviously from India – has a red mark on her forehead."

"Oh." He went back to reading his paper.

His response gave her pause yet her enthusiasm prevailed. "Want to go?"

He looked at her and sighed. "Don't you think you're going out on a tangent lately? Reading all those hocus books and going to witchy-type lectures?"

Whoa. She shivered at his use of the witch word. She got it; he was afraid of the spiritual realm. She gently stroked his arm. "Okay, so you're not into this stuff. Don't worry, I won't push it on you."

Charlie put his paper aside. "In the culture I grew up with, there was black magic; hocus-pocus I call it. People sticking pins into dolls. Revenge. Curses. Even educated people do it. I don't want any part of it."

"Oh God, me neither." She understood. Tension clutched her stomach. This was the first time they'd been out of sync about anything big. She needed to think alone. "I'll get dinner going."

She peeled an onion and started chopping. Poor Charlie. How awful to be around that type of superstition. Curses that caused fear brought all sorts of bad luck. Black magic. What a horrible mind trick. Judas Priest!

Silvia chopped so hard, the onion turned to mush. She considered pulling out a new one, then decided the onion mash would add more flavor to the chicken. Her throat tightened. If she continued her pursuit, it might cause a rift with Charlie.

Wait a minute. It was not *her* fear. Charlie had to get over it. What she was doing had nothing to do with black magic. Despite his disapproval, she was going to hear this woman.

On Saturday morning the bus was nearly empty. Too excited to sit down, Silvia grabbed the handle grip. Her heart thumped loudly. Why the excitement? Did her heart know something her brain did not?

When she stepped off the bus, the bright sun squinted her eyes and softened the cold air on her face. She wanted to run, but dignity slowed her to a fast walk for the few blocks to the Jung Society building. The red-brick complex had a welcoming feel with its white trim and bright red doors. Her intuition signaled something very important was about to happen.

Silvia joined a crowd of mostly women who moved slowly through the doors. They followed signs that said, A Public Program of Self-Realization by Shri Mataji Nirmala Devi. Silvia's breath quickened. A tiny fear that this could be another worthless trip flew out the window. This woman would do more than just talk.

Typical of Washington, D.C. the group was mixed; white, black, Asian, Latin American and a group dressed in colorful African dashikis. The presence of only a few men in the crowd – who all appeared to be accompanying a woman – reinforced her belief that females are more spiritually aware than males. In this realm, women need to lead the way. A healthy society depends on it.

Eager to get as close as possible to the speaker, Silvia sped up and wove dexterously around the slow movers. When she slid into the one remaining front row seat, she smiled triumphantly. Finally settled, she took a deep breath and caught a whiff of her roll-on deodorant mixed with perspiration. She hoped her neighbors wouldn't catch the scent.

Some of her anxiety disappeared when she spotted the roses, lilies, chrysanthemums and daisies artfully arranged on the stage. Such grandeur caused her to give a silent thank-you to whoever did the flowers, grateful for the calming effect. A large graph stood on an easel beside the podium. It looked like a simplified drawing of the central nervous system, with various circles dissecting the spine. The scientific look gave her hope the information would be grounded in the practical; not flaky and esoteric. Her desire for useful knowledge had reached a fever pitch.

A hush filled the hall as all eyes followed a young East Indian man as he stepped up to the podium. He tapped the mic a few times. In a cheerful British accent he said he was pleased to see that so many wanted to meet the Divine Mother, which he explained was an English translation of her spiritual name.

Silvia's heart continued to throb heavily.

"Born sixty years ago in India into a Christian family, she studied medicine, became a wife and mother, and now a grandmother. She knew from childhood that her job this lifetime was to give self-realization to humanity. In her early years she was an active supporter of Mahatma Gandhi in his nonviolent struggle to free India from British rule."

Silvia's attention honed in on the name. Not only was Gandhi her hero, but it meant the Divine Mother was a political activist. A kindred soul. More adrenaline rushed into her face.

Finally, a beaming woman draped elegantly in a white sari with a red border, stepped briskly up to the platform. Her long black hair was parted in the middle of her widow's peak, highlighting large, soft eyes and full lips within a moon-shaped face that glowed. She stood at the microphone and surveyed the audience with smiling eyes. For one split second, her glance caught Silvia's. Whoa. A spark of recognition flared to life. Silvia clutched the arms of her chair and leaned forward.

With hands folded in a prayerful gesture, the Divine Mother bent slightly at the waist towards the audience. "I bow to all the seekers of truth." She paused, and glanced around the hall again.

"You have to know what the truth is. We cannot order it. We cannot manipulate it. We cannot organize it. It is what it is, has been and will be.

"And what is the truth?

"Truth is we are surrounded, penetrated, nourished, looked after and loved by a very subtle energy which is the energy of divine love.

"The second truth is that we are not this body, this mind, these conditionings, this ego. But we are the spirit.

"The third truth is that an intelligent, enlightened energy sleeps inside every human's sacrum bone." She said she was here today to wake it up for those who have the desire.

"When activated, the energy goes against gravity as she travels up through the central nervous system and cleans away negativity in her path." She pointed to the middle channel on the chart.

"Her destination is to pierce through the top of our heads at the soft spot we had as babies. Her goal is to connect us to the all-surrounding energy of divine love." She gestured upwards with her hands.

"Once you are connected, she works with you like a mother and you are her only child. Gradually her powerful energy will cleanse you of negativity that prevents you from being your most healthy, happy, highest self. If you work with her a little every day, the truth will reveal itself to you. The truth is you are beautiful spiritual beings."

Silvia's attention wandered in and out of the multiple threads the Divine Mother wove in her talk. Something was moving inside, gently massaging the knots in her stomach. As pressure subsided, a blissful sensation took its place.

She was enveloped in a coolness that seemed to come from the Divine Mother. This treatment – or whatever it was – felt more important to her than mentally understanding the lecture. The energy was soothing like Elwood's, but hugely more robust.

At the end of the talk, the Divine Mother invited questions. This portion went too long for Silvia. Impatience took over. Like a spoiled brat, she folded her arms in front of her chest and silently begged to have the experience, not the talk, talk, talk.

Finally the Divine Mother announced that those who still had questions could save them until after realization. "I will guide you through a meditation to enable you to wake up your own sleeping energy. And once it's active in you, you can awaken it in someone else. It's like a burning candle passing its light to another."

A deep calm oozed over Silvia. When the something moving inside reached her forehead, tears sprang from her closed eyes. A dam had burst. The energy plowed through and magically removed some debris in its path. Her usual steady stream of thoughts subsided.

The Divine Mother continued. "Place your right hand on top of your head and press your palm where the soft spot was. Now slowly massage the scalp to loosen it."

Silvia complied, hoping her's wasn't too calcified.

"This powerful energy, which can pass through anything, is now ready to flow out of your head and make the connection. But that cannot happen against your will. So if you want this, inside yourself say, 'please give me my self-realization.' "

Silvia pleaded for the breakthrough. Her intuition was that the energy would take her into a higher realm of consciousness. Who wouldn't want that?

When the Divine Mother advised them to, Silvia removed her hand but kept her attention at the top of her head. A unique stillness engulfed her body. No thoughts, only bliss.

"Your attention is now above your mind. Notice how you have no thoughts but are still aware. You can hear the cars going by. You can hear the sounds of the city but you're not thinking. This state is called thoughtless awareness. You are now in meditation."

A Mozart symphony filled the hall, adding musical frequencies to the surging vibrations. For long moments no thoughts cluttered Silvia's mind as she effortlessly kept her attention on top of her head. She became aware of tensions being released from what seemed like every nerve, every organ, every cell in her body. She was drenched in peace.

When the Divine Mother told the audience to open their eyes, Silvia was reluctant. What if the bliss went away? Would she be able to get it back?

As if in response, the Divine Mother spoke. "I'll show you how to raise your kundalini quickly, so you can easily do this meditation at home. Kundalini is the Sanskrit name for this enlightened energy. You may have heard of it. It has been kept secret for thousands of years and very few people had it awakened. But in these modern times, we are well equipped to handle the power of Kundalini.

"Now that you have it active, it's important to meditate for as little as ten minutes a day to clean your subtle system and keep it clean. Otherwise, she will go back to sleep. A few of the more advanced meditators among you have booked a room in a public library where you can go to learn more and meditate together. This information is always provided free of charge because spiritual knowledge is the birthright of every human being."

She folded her hands in a prayerful gesture toward the audience. "Congratulations. You are now realized souls. Your health will improve. Your sensory perception of every living thing will expand. You are on an evolutionary path, moving from mere human to spiritual being. You will become a powerhouse of love."

The Divine Mother invited those who wished to speak with her to come on the stage. Eagerly Silvia joined the long line and watched as words were exchanged with each person. In some cases, she moved her hand in a circular motion outside various places on their bodies, as if to clear away invisible negativity. When Silvia's turn came, joy spontaneously bubbled up inside.

"Silvia, I'm so happy you came. I've been waiting for you. Did your children come with you?" The Divine Mother took Silvia's hand.

She knows me! Her answer came out in a whisper. "No, not this time."

"I'll be coming back soon, so then, please bring them with you." She put her hand a few inches over Silvia's head. "You really got it good, yes?"

The powerful energy swirling around intensified. "Yes, I feel so much joy!"

"The joy – yes – your spirit's giving it to you. Joy. That's the quality of the spirit." She folded her hands and bowed.

Back home, Silvia waited for the kids to arrive. Strong vibrations had settled inside and she noticed – maybe for the first time in her life – her stomach area felt completely relaxed. When she looked at the photo of the Divine Mother she'd picked up at the event, a flow of cool energy wafted across her hands. Not as strong as the Mother's in person, but the photo worked as a catalyst; the energy flowed into her brain. No marijuana or alcohol high came close to the bliss she felt when her attention went above the words that otherwise spewed through her mind nonstop.

Marilyn came in and saw Silvia with hands open towards a photo. Silvia quickly pulled her hands away and smiled sheepishly.

"So what's this about?" Marilyn was an intelligent, kind human being, yet Silvia hesitated, uncertain where to begin. Marilyn made it easier. "Tell me about the photo."

Silvia gestured for Marilyn to sit beside her. "Since you're a scientific type, you know that photography captures the cellular alignment of whoever's in the picture, right?" Marilyn nodded. "You also know that our cells emit vibrations – some positive, some negative – usually mixed and occasionally balanced. But in most normal people they're pretty weak, so we don't feel them when we look at a photo."

"Agreed," she said.

"Okay, so . . . hold out your hands a minute in front of this photo, palms up." Silvia waited thirty seconds. "Feel anything?"

Marilyn looked down at her hands. "Maybe – on my palms. Cool air blowing?"

"Yes, that's it. Those are vibrations. Cool means good, warm means there's some problem. So this woman is so full of these good vibes that even her photo works like a divine utility that boosts your own vibrations. But in person, wow! She radiates spiritual energy so strong everyone around her can't help but smile. It feels so good.

"Sounds awesome. How can I get it?"

Silvia was about to explain when footsteps came thundering up the stairs. "We're here!" Frankie, Linda and Alan burst into the room, plopped their overnight bags on the floor and huddled around Silvia.

"I'll leave you guys alone, "Marilyn said. "We can get back to this later."

When the kids were settled, Silvia asked them to sit on the floor with their legs crossed. "I just learned how to wake up some new energy that sleeps inside. Let's find out if yours is awake." They didn't resist. She lifted her open palms outside their backs to raise their energy. "Now put the palm of your hand flat on your head. Then up . . . up . . . little higher." She positioned their hands above what was the soft spot. "Now see if you feel anything."

Alan was first to say he felt wind. The others agreed. Silvia smiled, pleased they got it so quickly. No doubt they were so young they hadn't collected a lot of negativity to block the way.

Then caution took over. She thought of Frank. He might react like Charlie – with fear – if he knew she involved them in something spiritual. It could jeopardize their weekends together. She easily diverted their attention. "Who wants to go for a bike ride?"

It wasn't until the kids had gone that she phoned Charlie. She wondered if she should tell him about the most profound experience of her entire life. But he didn't ask about the lecture, so she didn't tell.

She had just hung up the phone when Marilyn came in, eager to pick up where they left off. Silvia used the Divine Mother's method and took her through the awakening. When Marilyn announced she felt the bliss, chills tingled inside Silvia. She had successfully passed the torch.

If only the men in her life were as easy. Her stomach churned when she reflected on why she didn't tell Charlie. Was this the beginning of the end?

On Monday morning, the Unity House team met at George Hardy's law firm to choose which candidates to put forward for FCC commissioner. The fact that she and Charlie were a couple had become public knowledge, so they could greet each other warmly, briefly touching hands, since neither was up for kissing in public.

John, George, Brad and Charlie had already culled a list of candidates down to three, all men. There was a lawyer from New Orleans, a telecommunication engineer from D.C., and another lawyer who was also a minister, from Tennessee. This would be the first black person to sit on the FCC over its entire thirty plus years of existence, so it was important to make sure the candidates were squeaky clean. A decision was made to hire professional investigators to vet them thoroughly – rule out immoral, illegal or corrupt noise of any kind. They'd have to withstand the scrutiny of senate confirmation hearings.

The meeting was about to end when George got a call. He left the room to take it but returned in a few minutes. His tone was bitter. "You all know how we've been patting ourselves on the back for having killed Jacob's S.2004 bill? Well, the FCC just resurrected it. They've issued a policy statement that says the same thing; the public riffraff cannot be involved nor hassle us in any way at renewal time of our buddies' broadcast licenses."

Anxiety gripped Silvia. Worried looks were exchanged.

"Goddamn it!" John blurted out. "Can they do that legally?"

George scowled, red-faced. "They have discretionary powers when it comes to license renewal. They can make rules without even issuing a notice to the public. They don't have to take any outside comments. So yeah, they can do it."

"We can block them with a restraining order," Charlie said. "A judge will have to consider our request even if they eventually throw it out. It'll buy us some time."

George nodded. "Good. Let's get right on it. John, you and Brad could help us with some of the language if you can stay for a few more hours?"

It was agreed that Lisa and Silvia would hightail it back to Unity House to warn the others preparing to file petitions. Within a few hours, black leaders in Detroit, Memphis, Dallas, Chicago, Boston, Indianapolis, Rochester, and Columbus were advised not to be confused nor discouraged nor stopped nor delayed in any way by any policy statements. The nationwide blitz of petitions was crucial to bring their local stations to the negotiating table. To bolster their confidence, Lisa and Silvia shared the breaking news that the D.C. station whose license had been petitioned, within a few weeks created an on-the-job training program for black and other minority students.

When the calls were finished, Silvia and Lisa sat down for a coffee and cigarette break.

"All the people I talked to are still gung ho," Lisa said.

"Yep, mine too." After taking a few drags, Silvia put out her cigarette. "Yuck. That tastes awful."

Lisa's eyes widened. She stared at Silvia for a few moments. "Yeah, what's with you? You look different."

"How so?"

"Um . . . I don't know. But something's changed."

"I sure feel different. It's a long story." She wasn't sure how to describe her transformation in a way that Lisa wouldn't think she was weird.

"We have time. What happened?"

She minimized the story to the fact that everyone has a dormant energy system in the sacrum bone that can be awakened. Hers was now active, and it felt like a heavy flow of love massaged her insides. And her senses, like taste, were registering more info; as if open wider. "The most exciting thing it gives me is a steady state of joy, like I had when I was a little kid." She smiled and took a deep breath. "It's goes beyond any high I ever felt."

Lisa gave Silvia her skeptical look. "You're not telling me everything. You can do better. You're a trained journalist. Tell all."

Silvia chuckled. There was no way to keep anything from Lisa. "You could get words out of the deaf and dumb." She told Lisa the whole story about the Divine Mother, what she looked like, what she said, how Silvia felt afterwards. "And I can awaken yours too, if you want."

Lisa poured herself another cup of coffee and lit another cigarette. "Ahh . . . no." She exhaled. "Guess I'm not ready yet. I'll keep watch and see what happens."

"Chicken."

"Yes, I am and want my cigarettes to keep tasting good."

"Oh God. I can see what I'm in for. If you only watch, madam inspector, you won't know what it feels like inside. You'll miss out on a super high."

Lisa responded with her usual dry sense of humor. "I'll be on the look-out for any tricks you might try" – she flung one arm upward – "like levitating to the ceiling. I know you'll do anything to prove your point."

A few days later, Silvia finally told Charlie about her experience. He studied her eyes and face, as if checking to see if she'd been mesmerized. His only comment was that he hoped she wouldn't try to convert him.

On the other hand, when she told John and Elwood what happened, John said he was glad she found what she was looking for. But he had Elwood and didn't need anything more in the spiritual realm.

Elwood told her she'd changed. "Your aura is fuller and brighter now that some of your kundalini's flowing." Silvia felt proud and did a slight curtsey.

He frowned. "Don't let your ego blow up. Notice I said some; there's one-thousand strands; you have only a few active."

"What? Why not one thousand?"

"Because your central nervous system isn't all cleared of the grunge in there. It has to clean out all your organs...stuff that's been in there since your beginning. It's little by little each time you meditate."

Silvia's alarm showed in the loudness of her voice. "That could take years!"

Elwood laughed. He patted her arm. "Ah my dear, you have yet to learn patience. It used to take decades of purification before any seeker was rewarded with realization. But now the Divine Mother cleared the way to awaken the kundalini easily for anyone that wants it. Doesn't matter how much they misbehaved. To clean themselves, all they have to do is use it to meditate a little bit every day. No one else in the history of life on the planet has ever been able to awaken the kundalini of the masses."

Elwood paused and gave Silvia a stern look. "Just because you got it so easily, don't take it for granted."

Silvia *was* changing. The more sludge her meditation cleared out, the more disturbed Charlie became. "You're not even allowed to have a glass of wine. No smoking. Hardly any swearing. Aren't you becoming a fanatic?"

"Charlie, do you think I'm that stupid? No one's telling me to stop anything. I keep trying to drink. But each time, the alcohol takes away my high. It makes me depressed. I can feel my forehead being clogged. Why in hell would I want to lose my high?"

"I'm not looking for a high when I drink. Just to relax. Forget my problems."

"Okay, but it's not like I have to discipline myself not to take a drink. The desire's gone. And you never liked me to smoke anyway, so why aren't you glad about that?"

"I'm glad you're not smoking anymore. But I don't like the reason you quit."

She wanted to laugh out loud at his illogic, but his face looked too grim. She tried another tactic. "This energy makes it easy to change the things I don't like about myself. It's as simple as using a hose to clean away mud. I wish you'd at least give it a try."

"No way. I'm sorry you have so many things you don't like about yourself." He jumped up and stomped to the window.

Interesting. He never looks at himself so of course, he's a perfect person.

After a few uncomfortable moments, he came back, sat beside her and lifted one of her hands. He traced the backs of her fingers.

"Sorry. I didn't mean that like it sounded."

He pulled her close. Silvia didn't resist.

"So let's just continue like it is, you drinkin' a Coke while I drink my beers."

Silvia faked a laugh. She used to enjoy their political and philosophical discourse over a glass of wine. Over many glasses. That was one of the reasons she fell for Charlie. But now the conversations were less interesting when she was clearheaded and his brain was slurry.

Silvia became fast friends with others who attended regular meditations. They connected spirit-to-sprint; conversational depth was instant. They shared the joy of new sensory awareness and swapped stories about their changes.

One change they all had in common was being able to detect swelling of their left temple – as if their hair was being lightly pulled – usually when angry; always during arguments. In an audio talk, the Divine Mother explained it was the ego inflating from excessive heat, caused by the anger, that travels up the right sympathetic. "It crosses at the optic chasm, and inflates the ego like a balloon. The balloon then blocks your kundalini from connecting to the – what I call – the divine internet. Disconnected, your objectivity is gone; reason no longer prevails."

For Silvia, being able to detect her ego's state was a powerful tool. If she caught herself in time, she'd stop arguing or whatever she was doing when it inflated. She could deflate the balloon if she gave a gentle smack to tamp the damn thing down. Her ego was too easily inflated. Maybe other people had this problem, so why didn't the Creator make it visible? What if people could see the ugly yellow balloons floating above each other's heads? Maybe tongues would be held and wars prevented.

Silvia's esteem for the Divine Mother continued to grow when she heard taped lectures about issues she cared about; racism, materialism, extreme aggression, and religious fanaticism. But when the Divine Mother described the lack of chastity as a primary cause of ill health, Silvia became alarmed. What did lack of chastity have to do with disease?

She had decided since she and Charlie were both divorced, living together was a good idea. With all the broken marriages nowadays, it seemed practical to run a test – research each other's foibles – before taking the vows.

On the other hand, she had just uncovered her subtle but continuous fear about Charlie's commitment to their relationship. This nagging concern pushed a truth into her attention. A truth she well knew. *Fear on the part of a researcher distorts the results.*

More distress filled her brain. She was convinced that one possible cause of her cancer could be from the sustained period of fear and anxiety around the divorce. She knew for certain anger and fear can cause cells to bloat. The swollen cells can clump into growths that disrupt cellular communication which can become cancerous.

That did it. Serious doubt about the health of sleeping with Charlie took hold.

The weather was sunny yet pleasantly cool when B.E.S.T. members and supporters gathered for a family picnic in Rock Creek Park. Silvia and the kids arrived to delectable smells from sizzling barbeque that saturated the pavilion area. Frankie sprinted off to join the football game, while the younger two raced for the swings. Silvia spotted Ashton in a chef's apron standing over a smoking grill.

"Hey! Yum . . . so you're in charge of the burgers. Need any help?"

Ashton handed her the spatula. "Yeah, take over. I'll be right back with more."

Silvia scanned the area. There was a mob of what looked like elders – gray haired people – who sat in lawn chairs beside a make-shift stage. She recognized some Unitarian friends and others from Ashton's organization. A larger group of adults mingled with paper cups around a table with several kegs of beer and cases of soda. Fifty or so kids of all ages were scattered around the playground. The turnout was huge.

Once the food supply dwindled to scraps on the meat trays and a few crumbs of cake, the kids went back to their games and the adults moved to the stage area. Silvia wasn't involved with the hosting team so wondered what was supposed to happen next. She found Charlie, Lisa and Brad and they joined the crowd of onlookers.

Ashton stepped up to the microphone. "Hope everyone has a full belly . . . how'd you like the food?" The crowd shouted their approval. "Okay good! Good!"

He had removed his apron to reveal a black tee shirt with 'BEST' blazed in white across his chest. Silvia and Lisa had not known such shirts existed and spoke excitedly about where to buy some for their kids. Others next to them joined the conversation until Ashton gave them an annoyed look. "If I can have your attention here please, I'd like to begin." Everyone shushed.

"Welcome to the first Black Efforts for Soul in Television awards party. I know you're wondering how come we chose a family picnic in the outdoors and not inside a fancy hotel. For one thing, we didn't want to be tortured by rubber chicken and uptight clothes. We knew somewhere that felt more like home would be just fine with you all."

The audience clapped their approval.

Ashton's face become serious; his tone louder. "But don't think this casual setting means what we are here to celebrate is trifling. No! What we are here to celebrate is enlightened. We have increased the ability of the people of this nation to engage more fully into brotherly love!"

The crowd stood up and clapped, cheered and shouted "yes! yes!" until Ashton quieted them. He introduced Harry Pine to make the awards. Harry hopped onto the stage and waved to the crowd.

"Ladies and gentlemen, today we celebrate Black Efforts for Soul in Television. Through their ingenious campaign, this non-violent, grass roots, mostly volunteer network has begun the take down of the walls of prejudice and opened our nation's media to reflect the true racial diversity that makes America beautiful. No question about it, a revolution of the American soul is underway.

"You all know most of the details of how – using legal tactics – these B.E.S.T warriors bombarded the nation's TV stations with license renewal threats. The blitz got even bigger when advocates for Spanish speakers, Orientals, women and children got wind of the strategy and jumped onto the petition band wagon. And it worked! Today nearly every station petitioned has created training, employment and relevant programs that include everyone.

"The crowning jewels are the thousands of black students who reported to B.E.S.T that they are preparing themselves for careers in the TV industry. In the near and distant future, we will have producers, directors, news anchors, journalists, show hosts, and heroes and heroines who are black on all the networks.

"So, who sparked all of this?" Harry scanned the crowd. "John Darnell please come up here."

The audience went wild. They stood. They cheered. They applauded until Harry stopped them.

Totally unaware that this would happen, John's face lost color and his body trembled as he climbed up on the stage. His reaction flooded Silvia with anxiety for him, until finally he smiled and faced the crowd.

Harry put his arm around John. "Don't worry. We're not going to make you give a speech. We want you to know how grateful we are for your wisdom that enabled this strategy to morph into a revolution."

He kept his arm around John and turned towards the audience. "When the idea was first brought to his attention, John helped it germinate and then grow and grow until the strategy was strong and secure. He sought out and joined forces with the necessary expertise. He did not covet the how-to-do-it information like some executives who think they must control information. Instead he reached out to his contacts in major cities and excited them into action. To give them the deeper, legal knowledge, he deployed his staff to create guidelines and conduct workshops. John, the warrior that he is, never hesitated to put himself on the front lines. When the industry went to congress to kill the petition drive, John and his team fought back and won. Then the FCC tried to kill the drive with a policy trick. John and his team fought back again, and again they won. Thanks to everyone who played a role, and are still fighting the good fight, our public airwaves have begun to reflect the reality of a racially diverse America."

Harry picked up a trophy from a nearby table. "So on behalf of all of us, John, we present you with this twenty-four carat gold sparkplug mounted on an oak wood plaque that says, 'To John Darnell, the Catalyst that Sparked a Revolution.'"

After all the accolades and jokes about John being a spark plug, he took over the mic and honored the Unity House staff and volunteers. When called, Silvia stood beside the others and smiled broadly, deeply privileged to have played a role.

After the ceremony, Brad took the stage to ask the B.E.S.T. activists to keep the pressure on for a black FCC commissioner. He reminded that President Nixon had reneged on his promise to nominate a black person the last time an opportunity arose. "At the last minute, he changed his mind and added a woman to the all male commission. Of course, she was white."

The next day a rollicking touch football game was underway in the front yard at Silvia's place. Linda and Frankie made up one team, Alan and Silvia another. There was a lot of laughter about the rules, as illegal tackling and holding were allowed. The game was tied when Frankie threw a pass. Linda would have caught it for the touchdown, except from out of nowhere, a small black boy ran onto the field. He intercepted the pass, cradled the ball and ran across the street, skillfully dodging traffic. The kids took off after him. Cars honked. Traffic stopped. No one got hit, but the ball stealer got away.

Frankie was furious. "He can't do that – it's our ball!" He pounded his fist into his hand.

"Yeah," Linda agreed. "Let's go find him."

Alan was so shaken, he began to cry. Silvia put her arms around him. "It'll be okay. Let's go inside and get some juice and cookies. Then we'll go looking for that boy."

As they refreshed themselves, Silvia realized the incident could be used to show her children, up close, how some people lived with less material wealth. "I wonder why he didn't just ask to join us, like any kid where you live would have. Do you think he thought we might not let him play? Or do you think he just wanted the ball?"

"He wanted the ball," Frankie said.

"Yeah, maybe he doesn't have one," Linda said.

Or maybe he did it on a dare, Silvia thought. Steal from the rich to give to the poor. "Let's see what we find out."

She led the kids to the next block where she suspected the boy might live. None of the homes had been renovated. As they strolled down the sidewalk, they saw several black people sitting on their porches. Silvia nodded and waved hello, and they waved back. She was glad to find friendliness on a street that no doubt rarely had white people strolling by. Metal lawn chairs, bicycles and toys were strewn across some of the front yards.

"Kids live here," Frankie said, pointing out the toys.

Toward the end of the block, they caught sight of a group of black children. Frankie and Linda slowed down, shy to approach kids they didn't know. Silvia held Alan by the hand and walked confidently up to the group.

"Hi!" She smiled warmly. From their sizes, she surmised most were under ten. "Hey, we were playing touch football in our yard when somebody came and borrowed our ball. We're wondering if you'd like to come and play with us."

All looked surprised. They eyed each other, shifted their feet, and looked down. Their tension caused Silvia to know she had guessed correctly. They knew about the ball. Maybe had even dared the smallest boy to get it. It happened so fast she couldn't recognize who it was, especially since he wore jeans and a white T-shirt like all the other boys. She crouched down to their height and put her arm around the kid standing next to her. She kept smiling.

"Tell you what. You all bring the ball and come to our yard. We can choose up teams and have a game. What do you say?" She nodded up the street. "But you'll need to ask your parents first."

Frankie and Linda hung back. Silvia wished that instead of acting shy, they would second the invitation. She gave them a pleading look. "Their names are Frankie and Linda, and I'm sure they'd like to have more kids to play with. Yes?" Linda got the message.

"Sure," she said. Her voice was barely audible.

"And this here's Alan." Silvia kept up the chatter. "So what are your names?"

Finally the black children relaxed. One of the taller girls, who gave her name as Sheila, went around and pointed to each child, naming them. "I'd like to play football," she said. "I'll ask my mother if I can." Under Sheila's leadership, the others followed suit.

Silvia and her kids waited on the sidewalk while permission to go to the next block and play with a white family was sought. Without a word spoken by anyone, a football with the name Nolan printed in black ink on it, appeared in the arms of one of the boys. The troops followed Silvia as she led them to the playing field.

The game was rough – more tackle than touch, and skill sets were widely varied. Before anyone got seriously hurt, Silvia ended the game by inviting everyone in for juice and cookies.

"From now on," she said, "this football will be kept outside in the old milk box beside the front door. You can come and get it when you want to play, just remember to put it back when you're finished." The black kids looked at one another but said nothing.

When they had gone, Frankie said, "What if they take it again, and don't bring it back?"

Silvia looked at him thoughtfully and put her arm around his shoulders. In a tender voice, she suggested he probably knew the answer to his own question.

"Well, we do have other footballs – four or five of them at home. I'll bring another the next time we come, just in case."

Frankie got a hug. "Your generosity – it's a good thing."

After the kids had gone home, Silvia took a breath – the first quiet moment of the weekend. When she sat for meditation, she noticed an ache in her stomach. Immediately she knew the cause. Charlie. How would he react to her change of heart about making love out of wedlock?

8

Tension persisted between Silvia and Charlie. A few times, she faked fatigue when Charlie made overtures. But the third time, he ended her guise when he abruptly sat up and turned on the light.

"Let's not play games. What's going on?" His voice was shaky.

Silvia bolted upright. She felt guilty being too cowardly to tell him about her change of heart. When she saw the hurt glazing his eyes, tears welled up. God, how to explain? He would not understand. She shook her head. "Give me a minute."

He lay back down and crushed a pillow over his face. Compassion filled Silvia's heart and came out in her voice.

"It's nothing you've done wrong. Charlie, I feel so much love for you. It's just . . . well . . . sleeping with you like this and not being married, it doesn't feel healthy anymore."

Charlie lurched back up. "Oh God, now this. It's gone way too far." His voice grew louder. "Did this guru person tell you to do this? To shut me out? To stop sleeping with me?"

Silvia rubbed a calming hand down his arm. "It's totally coming from me, not her. Charlie, I know these changes are sudden. I'd react the same way if it was you doing this." She angled away from him, trying to find the right words. "I'll be honest with you. What's happening to me is like, like coming out of a dense fog. And I don't want to do things that put me back into it. Sleeping with you when you're not my husband makes fog for me. I know the difference. I once had a husband." She waved a hand through the air. "It's the same with the wine. This new sensitivity gives me joy, and doing all that other stuff takes it away."

Charlie's eyelids drooped, his mouth twisted. He sighed, but said nothing. Instead, he lay down and rolled over, turning his back to her.

Silvia slept little that night. Her mind raced with worry that her actions would be fatal to their relationship. She was relieved when she heard Charlie snoring. At least her decision did not bother his sleep.

In the morning, still groggy, she shuffled into the kitchen and found Charlie up, dressed and already drinking coffee. She hoisted herself onto a bar stool.

"Good morning!" He handed her a mug of coffee and eased onto the stool beside her. With a twinkle in his eye, he said, "I have a proposition for you."

Hmm. Was he going to ask her to marry him? She nodded for him to go ahead.

"I'd like to take some time to investigate your newfound religion. Then when I'm ready, I'll present my findings, for you to do with them what you like. Would you agree to consider the results of my research? "

Her shoulders drooped. She tilted her head down to hide disappointment. So why was he so energized? He must be certain the Divine Mother's program is a con and that he'd nail it as such and she would back off.

"Okay, okay." She slipped off the stool and went to the sink. She stared at the drain. Her throat tightened. "But don't call this a religion. Or if you want to call it that, you should know it's a natural one. It's inside everyone." She took a long breath and sighed, trying to hide her annoyance. "So take as much time as you want. But, Charlie, in the meantime, I think I'd better sleep at my own place until we both get straight about where we're going with this." Nervous about her boldness and his answer, she felt perspiration break out on her neck. When he didn't speak, she pushed for an answer. "What do you think?"

He moved next to her and gently pulled her into his arms. "You do what you want. I believe we both want this to work out, so let's get on with it."

Relieved that he didn't seem upset, she lingered in his arms until he pushed her away. "No fair making this difficult for me." He winked at her. "Be kind." Then he grabbed his coat and briefcase, waved goodbye and went off to work.

Two weeks later, Charlie announced he was ready to present. He pulled a bar stool over in front of the coffee table so he looked down on Silvia where she sat on the couch. He opened a folder and pulled out some letter-size photos. "One report calls it a cult. It says that her followers worship her feet. Here, you can see little children pouring water over them." He carefully placed the photos in front of her. "Notice they're wearing Indian clothes and have red marks on their foreheads."

He appeared to be struggling to keep his voice level.

"Um, yes." She respectfully studied the photos. "I've been to these worship services. It's hard to understand what's happening if you can't feel the vibrations."

His tone grew shrill. "They even let her tell them who they should marry, and of course it's always someone who worships her."

Charlie laid out several more photos of Western-looking women in saris and men in what looked like white pajamas. They sat on the ground facing the Divine Mother, who sat on a stage. He gave her time to study them before he spoke.

"For God's sake, do you really know what you're getting into? How do you know you're not being brain washed? Put into a trance? Maybe you're being robbed of your free will by some fake guru."

She was prepared for Charlie's findings. She had seen the criticisms of the Divine Mother's teachings in newspapers that were leery of anything Hindu or Muslim. She fully understood what any Western person might think if they were on the outside looking in. Words alone could not explain inner transformations. Yet she had to try her level best for Charlie's sake. She took a sip of Coke to ease her dry throat.

"Okay. I'll address each of your – um – issues. So it's your turn to sit here, and I'll take the stool."

They switched places. Charlie sat stiffly; his face was somber.

Silvia felt relaxed. "Charlie, you look like you're on the defensive. Come on. You have to open up enough to at least try to listen."

"Okay. Let me get a beer." He retrieved his drink and sat back down.

"First, I'll talk about the worship of her feet. To understand any of this you need to know that all people have vibrations flowing from their feet – sometimes cool which means pure or positive; sometimes warm or hot which means negative. Your central nervous system would enable you to feel those vibrations – the same way you can feel cold air from an air conditioner or heat from a fire – if you had your self-realization. Otherwise your system cannot detect that type of subtle energy.

Since I have the energy awakened, I can feel very cool, very strong air flowing from the Divine Mother's feet. That's why it tells in *The Bible* that Jesus stooped to wash the feet of saints. He was honoring the fact that they were realized souls, so the energy flowing from their feet was pure. There's no doubt cool, strong air flowed from the feet of Jesus. If you poured water on them – you'd get the benefit. That's powerful love that flows. It heals. It feels good."

She waited for Charlie's reaction. His body remained stiff but now his shoulders were hunched and his brow furrowed. "Does this make any sense to you at all?"

"Not really. But go on."

"When this spiritual energy is flowing, of course it permeates everything inside of us, including the heart and the brain. You can surmise that all your sensory perceptions would be heightened – quite a lot."

"If you say so." He crossed his arms in front of his chest.

"Charlie, come on. Open up to listen." She gestured. "Look at your arms."

Red-faced, he uncrossed his arms. "Go on," he growled.

"Okay, about the red mark on the forehead . . . that's red paste made of chemical elements, such as red turmeric and lime water, that support the immune system. In Asian countries it has multiple purposes and compositions. Some women use it to show they are married. The Divine Mother applies it like a shield to protect the optic chiasm." She touched the space slightly above her eyebrows." It's a vulnerable place where the two sympathetic channels cross in the central nervous system. Virus-like negativity tries to enter there. Since this area controls the eyes and some brain functions, it's good to keep it protected to prevent outside subtle negativity from getting in. Applying the red paste shield is a practical safeguard, like sun-screen, only more auspicious. It's not hocus-pocus."

Charlie took a sip of beer and stretched his arms out on the back of the couch. "Keep going. I'm open. See?" His body remained stiff.

"Okay. Next, the marriage thing. Mates are selected after dozens of vectors are researched. In India they consider Eastern astrology, education and income levels, height, weight and interests, like hobbies. They look at values. Like does the person have a global view of the world or a parochial one? Do they like politics, animals and nature? What about methods of child rearing, materialism and morality? Many things like that are considered. Personally, I think it's a better system. We've been choosing mates based on what we learn about each other through dating and sexual attraction. Seems we end up with a lot of divorces."

Charlie looked surprised. He rubbed his head. He took another sip of beer. His tone was agitated. "Talk about the cult thing."

Now Silvia's anger came on hot and fast. She frowned. Her neck and shoulders stiffened, and she coughed to clear her throat. "*Cult.* Such an ugly word. All groups that had anything to do with the spirit were called that at one time or another. Catholics, Methodists, most protestant sects – you name them. But maybe your real fear is that we are all being mesmerized. Isn't that right? With your fear of witchcraft and hocus-pocus, you're worried that someone's bewitching us."

Her cool was blown, so she let her anger flow.

"Frankly, I'm insulted. How can you think that I'd join some cult? It's like you're saying I don't have the discretion or sensibility to know better. I'm not a person of low self-esteem or lack of confidence or needy for someone to always hold my hand and let me lean on them. Or is that how you see me?"

She stopped talking and glared at Charlie. She waited for an answer. He looked away and kept silent.

"You know, Charlie, it's one thing if you don't want to get involved in this meditation. But it's a whole other ball game if you don't respect it."

An uneasy silence filled the room. Charlie eventually broke it.

"So what are you saying? If I don't respect something you're doing that's turning you against me, *I'm* the bad guy?"

She was surprised to hear that. "Charlie, what do you mean about turning against you? The changes I'm going through are really good. I'm becoming a better person. It's not about you, not at all. Can't you see that?"

When Charlie spoke, his voice was choked. "What I see is you not wanting to be with me anymore."

"You mean not drinking and smoking pot with you?"

Her sarcasm made matters worse, and silence hung heavy.

"I mean – let's be honest, babe – you're pulling away. And if I don't join you in these changes, well, it'll be over for us." Before she could say anything, he added, "That's it, isn't it? I join you, or we're through?"

She sat down beside him and put her hand on his arm. She stopped herself from voicing her hope: *please join me.*

He pulled his arm away and slid apart, but his focus stayed on her. He stared at her for some moments. She could feel his anxiety entangled with hers. Then he got up and paced around the living room and into the kitchen. On his way past the refrigerator, he pulled out another beer and then moved back to the couch. He flopped down and after a heavy sigh took a long swig.

"I listened to all of what you said. And I do respect that you are really into this thing, whatever you call it. But at this stage of my life, I'll be honest. There's no way I'll ever respect it. It's too alien for me. Maybe I'm just not ready for self-realization." He leaned forward and put his head in his hands.

He took a few moments before facing her. "I do love you, but not enough to go off in that direction." He lowered his head. "I've made my decision." His voice was raspy, as if he had to force out his words. "It's over."

Sometimes the pain of truth hurts like a knife blade gorging the heart. Silvia sobbed continuously as she packed up her belongings. It wasn't until she was ready to go that she looked at Charlie. Tears fell down his cheeks and his face. His shoulders were crimped as he struggled to control his emotions. He kissed her on the forehead.

Too choked up to speak the words, they signaled goodbye.

The pain from their breakup was eased because they didn't see each other for one month. Then one morning Charlie appeared at Unity House, having been summoned by John for a meeting. When Silvia saw him, she was glad that her heart didn't pound or her face flush. Apparently, his reaction was equally level as he merely squeezed her hand, nodded and went directly into John's office.

Silvia didn't have time nor inclination to get bogged down in uncomfortable emotions. She had to read through the staggering barrage of mail from students who wanted TV careers and sort to fit the form letter responses she and Lisa had devised to handle the volume.

When Charlie emerged from his meeting, she patted the chair next to her. They studied each other for a few seconds. She saw that his face was peaceful. "So you're okay?" she asked.

"I'm okay. You too?"

"I'm good."

He put out his hand for her to shake. She shook it, tilted back her head and laughed. He laughed with her, stood, waved goodbye and left.

A wave of sadness passed over her when she turned back to the pile of mail. She started to muse over the sweet memories with Charlie. But now she knew how to control her attention and watched it constantly. If she didn't bring it back to the present, she would go into a depression. She quickly put her palm on the top of her head and held it until her attention was firmly there. Some minutes later, less overloaded by emotions, she could think clearly. What just happened?

Ah ha! The depression monster was demolished before it lured her into the dark side. She felt a warm glow of triumph to have tamed that particular beast.

9

A month passed by and summer blessed America's children with a vacation from school. Silvia and her kids sat on the back porch steps drinking lemonade after a sweaty badminton game. "Hey, guys, remember me telling you about the Divine Mother? She wants to meet you. We get to ride a bus to American University tonight. We'll go early enough to have dinner – they have a great cafeteria – and then – "

"Does that mean we have to sit through some speech?" Frankie's suspicions were aroused.

"Frankie, it'll be the first time you've ever been to a university. Do you even know what that is?"

"Sure, it's a school. A big one." His tone said *so what*? "Can't we go to the movies?"

Adventures that would delight all three kids used to be easy for Silvia, who was proud of her well-honed child-diplomacy skills. But now Frankie had accumulated ten years' worth of wisdom so had begun to question authority. If she was to gain everyone's cooperation now, she often had to use bribery and threats, not just sweetness. "It's an interesting place. They have a huge gym, basketball courts, a swimming pool – "

That excited Frankie. "Can we go swimming?"

"We can check it out, but without a membership . . . oh, guess what? They have ice cream and cake at the cafeteria. We can have both for dessert!" That tipped the young ones into cheers of happiness, and Frankie gave up his resistance.

Their arrival at the lecture hall was carefully orchestrated to be only minutes before start time which prevented the kids from the torture of sit-still-and-wait. Surprisingly, they kept their attention on the Divine Mother throughout the program. Silvia guessed it was due to the tranquilizing vibrations that filled the hall. When it was time to go onto the stage, the children's faces were radiant. Each was greeted by name, as if she had known them all their lives. Silvia was no longer surprised by that; she had seen the astonished faces of others when the Divine Mother spoke their names.

Silvia had other experiences that made her certain of the Mother's omni-presence. The first time was when she telephoned to ask Silvia to let the other meditators know about her return trip to D.C. in mid-June. When the conversation turned to personal niceties, the Divine Mother causally gave the location of a briefcase Silvia thought she had lost. Sure enough, as revealed, the case had slipped under a box of toys in the playroom. A few weeks later she phoned with her arrival details and told Silvia she liked her poetry, ". . . especially the one about ringing the bells for Mother Mary." Silvia was floored! She'd never shared her poetry with anyone.

When the Divine Mother finished with the children, she turned to Silvia. "I'm aware of the work you do to help rid your country of racism. The indigenous American people have suffered as much as the blacks since being robbed of their land and way of life. Most of them were born realized, but they don't know it nor do they know how to use kundalini to heal themselves. It would be good if you went to an Indian reservation to share the knowledge. Would you be willing?"

Excitement and possibility filled Silvia. She stammered. "I . . . I . . . I would be honored!" But how am I qualified?"

The Divine Mother smiled and took hold of Silvia's hands. "Just teach the way you learned. Talk to Dakotah. He'll know what to do."

Of course Dakotah was known to the Divine Mother. Apparently she knew everyone, and everything.

She turned her attention back to the children. "I need your mother to do some work away for a while. Will you be okay without her for a few months?"

"I'll be okay," Frankie said. Linda and Alan copied his words.

She hugged each child and said, "God bless you."

On the bus ride home, the children, in a rare state of calm, sat with eyes glued to scenes of the city at night passing by. Their quiet gave Silvia space to wonder about the mystical ways of divinity. Suddenly she jerked upright. Those words that came to her from deep inside when she was only eleven years old – was it the Divine Mother? It must have been – who else could have steered her to fight for racial justice?

Shivers fluttered up her spine.

When Frank picked up the kids, Silvia made no mention of the excursion. She decided it was wiser to wait and hear what the children would tell him about the Divine Mother. If he was upset, he would call and demand to know more.

She sprawled across an easy chair in the living room to wait for Dakotah to come home. What if he thought the idea was nuts; or worse, was insulted by the audacity of a white person telling the most spiritual people on the planet they needed more knowledge.

When Dakotah finally arrived it was late. Half hoping she'd have more time to gain courage, she told him she had to talk to him about something, but it could wait until morning if he was too tired.

He laughed. "What? You think I'm old? I'm never too tired. But I do need food and coffee." He led the way to the kitchen.

While Silvia made a fresh pot, Dakotah heated a bowl of leftover chicken and rice. When they had settled themselves at the table, Dakotah asked, "So what's up?"

His open hearted, casual presence had already put her at ease. "Well, it's about the changes you said you'd seen in me. I need to tell you how I got them."

His mouth full of food, he nodded for her to continue.

"It came from an Asian Indian who is filled with spirit – like the White Buffalo Calf Woman. She came to earth to connect those who are not connected to their inner spirit. So I learned from her and now I can feel it – the Great Spirit – everywhere." She looked down, feeling shy.

Dakotah waved his fork in the air. "You mean you never felt this before now?" Silvia heard the surprise in his voice. Her face flushed.

"No. Never. And I think most white people don't. It's only now that I can feel a physical connection with, as you say, Mother Earth and Father Sky. I think I'm becoming like you spiritually. Like all natives."

They looked at each other in silence. Strong energy pulsed between them. Dakotah tilted back his chair. "Do you think what she teaches could help my people?"

Silvia grinned. "No question. When you're finished eating, I'll give you the physical experience she gave us. You can decide for yourself."

When he was ready, he sat in a chair while Silvia stood behind him and moved her palms outside his spine, to raise his kundalini. Dakotah closed his eyes and became silent. With her palm above his head, she felt a jet of cool air.

Ten minutes later, he spoke very slowly. His voice was soft. "Never felt my power get so strong, so easily. Did she teach you how to use it to heal?"

"Oh yes." Silvia took a breath to slow down her words. "We learned how to feel where the clogs were in our central nervous system and how to remove them. Here, let me show you."

Dakota obviously had an innate sensitivity to vibrations in the nerves on his fingertips. He easily detected which organs in his body needed clearing. "The Divine Mother said you and your people were born with this energy awakened. Now I know it's true. It took me weeks of clearing out before I could feel what you felt instantly."

Silvia decided not to mention the Divine Mother's request yet. She wanted Dakotah to be convinced by his own experience that this was worth taking to the reservation.

Dakotah said he needed time to digest what he experienced. "Let's talk again tomorrow."

The next morning, Dakotah didn't waste time. "I hinted about this in the past, but now it's a formal invite. How'd you like to come and do some spiritual work on the reservation for a few months?"

"What? You mean live without all my comforts in extreme weather conditions?" Her broad smile revealed her delight. "Who wouldn't want to live among the most highly spiritual people in America? I am honored."

At Unity House, Silvia spoke to John as soon as he got in. "Could I get a leave of absence for a few months? Dakotah invited me to go to his reservation and teach them everything I've learned from the Divine Mother."

John's eyebrows shot up. He leaned back in his chair. "Two months? Why would it take so long?"

"Not sure. But if it's done sooner, you'll be the first to know."

"Charlie complains about the Divine Mother, you know. Now I may have to join him." He saw her alarm. "Just kidding. I don't want to be the bad guy and deny my Indian brethren a chance to heal." His eyes met hers and he winked. "Okay, girl, you go and do it. But be quick about it."

She telephoned Frank at work in hopes he would feel more at ease to talk there, away from the children's ears. When she asked if they told him about their time with the Divine Mother, his voice sounded relaxed. "They said she was like a soft, happy grandmother who knew all about them. Said she was really nice. Then they talked about ice cream and cake and an Olympic size swimming pool. What about it?"

"Did they tell you I'd be going away for a few months?"

"Nope. Are you? Where? When?"

"I am, and she's the reason. I mean, she asked me to go to an Indian reservation to show them what I learned from her about how to heal ourselves. One of my housemates is a Lakota – a lawyer who lives on the reservation – and runs a law project there. He's married with two children. I'll live in their home."

"Will you get paid?"

"Room and board. But I won't need money for anything. They'll pay my airfare back and forth."

"Why do they need you?"

Stress skittered into her chest. God, why was he asking so many questions? She thought for a moment, then realized he didn't sound hostile. She took a breath and hoped whatever came out of her mouth would not trigger any upset.

"Most Native Americans have spiritual energy that's awakened. We're all born with it, but in most of us it stays asleep our whole lives. But theirs was awake at birth and for many, it stayed that way. That's why they're so in tune with all living things, like nature. But they don't know how to use it to heal themselves. The Divine Mother showed me how and I can show them."

She waited for him to comment. When he didn't, she said, "That's all."

"Hmm. Okay. Give us your address and phone number when you know it. And, Silvia, you be careful."

For the first time since the split, there was warmth in his voice. How come? Was it because the divorce had come through? Months ago when the papers arrived in the mail, she was shocked. She had forgotten this was going to happen and was about to shove the papers out of sight into a drawer when she saw Frank's signature. Oh God! It's over. Sobbing, she quickly signed and mailed the papers back. But she never said a word about it to anyone.

Before she continued down this usual analytical path of what Frank might be feeling and why, she recognized this as one of her ridiculous behaviors she wanted to ditch. Instead, she chose to simply enjoy the fact that he sounded friendly.

When she explained to the kids that she would be gone for months on an Indian reservation where horses, buffalo, deer and antelopes roam, they all wanted to go along. "But I'll be busy every day teaching meditation stuff, and you'll be stuck just sitting and watching. Plus there's no ocean nor Chesapeake Bay and you guys get to go with your cousins to the beach for most of the summer."

The kids immediately backed down in favor of swimming, fishing and boating, like she knew they would. As they talked excitedly about their vacation, she realized they would hardly have a spare moment to think of her. So long away from them made her teary-eyed. She would miss out on chunks of their lives that could never be regained. Telephone calls would not fill the gaps as her kids were not interested in talking with people they could not see. Letters would help, but they wouldn't write spontaneously; Frank would have to give them a nudge.

She felt the mixed feelings of a soldier; eager to respond to a call of duty yet sad to leave the family behind.

10

On the flight to the reservation, Silvia learned more about Dakotah. He was born fifty years earlier, when the U.S. government was hell-bent on integrating Native Americans into the mainstream. At the tender age of four, the Federal Bureau of Indian Affairs took him away from his parents and put him into a church-run boarding school where the teachers used abuse – physical, including sexual and psychological – to fulfill the government's stated mission to take the Indian out of the children. Luckily, he was cunning enough to escape the worst of the abuse and smart enough to win a scholarship to the University of Colorado where he met his wife, Merry. After Dakotah graduated from law school and Merry completed a master's in journalism, the couple moved back to the reservation to use their skills to improve the lives of their people.

Dakotah was awarded grant money to finance a small legal team of one other lawyer, a technician, an investigator and a secretary. He said a lot of their cases were about domestic violence, drunk driving and drugs. But thanks to Merry's salary as a reporter for the *Big City Courier*, he could give pro bono time to fight the more complicated battles, such as racism, land rights and abuse of children by school officials.

On the drive through the reservation, Silvia was awed by the hundreds of acres of pristine grasslands, jagged red-rock mountains and endless skies. Occasionally a road, a cluster of small dwellings or a commercial building dotted the landscape. The dominance of nature and the clean air brought joy. But when they drove by ramshackle houses and shabby trailers with their look of poverty exacerbated by rusty abandoned cars, depression infiltrated the joy. Still, it was easy for a city dweller to appreciate the lack of asphalt, skyscrapers and traffic jams.

Dakotah's family home was a ranch rambler with painted gray siding trimmed in shiny white. Placed in the middle of several acres, it was surrounded by mowed grass and trees, patiently waiting to grow tall enough to provide shade. The house was named Project Place because it served as the law firm's work space as well as living quarters for the family and any team member that needed housing. It was one of very few large well-kept homes Silvia saw on the reservation, as most were small stuccos with outdoor pumps for water and outhouses for toilets.

On Monday morning, Silvia was delighted to be at the staff meeting.

"So first thing, let's deal with the elephant in the room," Dakotah said. He nudged Silvia. "Silvia here's a full-blooded white woman. I know her – she's good people. Lately she's become less of a wannabe and more like the real thing. Silvia, tell them what you told me about meeting up with an incarnation of the White Buffalo Calf Woman."

Silvia choked on her coffee while she scrambled upright. Her plan had been to not engage; only listen until she got a sense of everyone's personality. She was about to ask Dakotah to postpone her talk, but his deep, friendly look evaporated her resistance.

Since her spiel had not been worked out, she took advantage of the Lakota reverence for periods of silence during meetings, essential for thoughtful consideration of ideas. When she was firmly in tune with her intuition, she began.

"Racism is a white problem. So, as a white person, I'm an insider and can clue you in on some of the causes you may not know about. One of the biggest and most tragic causes is that many of us are spiritually retarded. Or maybe a better term is severely handicapped – or certifiably blind – spiritually." She surveyed the audience and felt friendly attention on her. She relaxed.

"I spent most of my life spiritually blind, although I always suspected there was a powerful something I didn't know about." She told them how she'd searched everywhere for whatever it was, until one day, very recently, it found her.

"It was the Divine Mother who came to Earth to awaken the spiritual energy coiled in every human's sacrum bone. Like all our organs, it was put there when we were in the womb. When it's awakened, it travels up the spine and goes out the top of the head to connect with the life force all around us. She connected me and that connection changed everything. I feel joy and inner peace deeper than anything I've ever felt before. All my senses are expanded. Now I hear, see, smell, taste; all with more detail. I can feel the Great Spirit is in every living thing – the trees, the ocean, the sky, the sun, the moon and of course, all people."

She paused and considered her audience. "So does it seem weird to you that I could have been so deprived? Spending thirty-five years without any awareness of the spirit inside me?"

Everyone looked blank; no one spoke.

"As natives, most of you were blessed to be born with your spiritual energy fully awake. You always felt the power inside yourselves and in all living things. So aren't you surprised that everybody doesn't have this awareness?" No one said anything. "Anyone?"

Dakotah leaned forward. "When you first told me about your awakening, I must admit I was thunderstruck. Wondered how anyone could go through life without having a relationship with the Creator." He smiled and looked down. Silvia appreciated his humility; a less kind person would have roared with laughter.

"The Divine Mother not only wakes up the energy, she teaches how to use it to diagnose and heal our physical, mental, and emotional problems." Silvia paused to see if there was any reaction. Their faces remained blank.

"Okay, so that's something you don't know yet. There are simple ways to use your own spiritual energy to overcome depression, insomnia and other imbalances. And once you've learned how to do it, you can teach it."

She smiled broadly. "So that's the story."

Dakotah got up and refilled his coffee mug. Everyone else looked down and then at each other.

"That was a good story," said the beautiful young woman who sat across the table from Silvia. The others nodded in agreement.

"Silvia, this here's Maya Flowers." Dakotah indicated the young woman whose long black hair framed a full-lipped smile and large brown eyes with thick, naturally dark lashes. "Her title on paper is secretary, but we call her our keeper. She keeps us happy, she keeps us accurately papered, and she keeps us on time." He went around the table introducing everyone.

There was Leonard, a bachelor – tall, handsome and muscular – fresh out of law school and eager to serve his people. And Sariah, a wife and mother who, with her tenacious investigative skills, never failed to provide whatever information they needed. And there was Big Eyes. Dakotah called him their fixer. "Computer problems, plumbing problems – he even holds our dilapidated passenger van together."

When the formal meeting ended and the social conversations began, Silvia was pleased by the warm welcome from each team member. She felt an immediate closeness like spirit-to-spirit. There were no walls between them.

At the end of her first week, Silvia was relaxing with Dakotah, Leonard and Big Eyes as they cheered and booed the Yankees vs. the Red-Sox game on TV. When the phone rang in the next room, Merry picked it up. They heard her high-pitched cries.

"Oh no, oh no. I'll be right over." She was crying, softly at first and then howling. Dakotah rushed to her side.

"Who?" he asked.

"Christy." She sobbed. "Hung herself. Tama found her in the bedroom." Merry's face was ashen. "I have to go to them."

"I'm going with you," Dakotah said.

Silvia could feel their agony. While she was in the dark about what happened, everyone else seemed to know. Big Eyes leapt up from the couch and asked Dakotah what they needed him to do. "We'll call from Tama's." His voice was calm but his face somber as he held Merry steady on the walk to the car.

When the couple had gone, Big Eyes and Leonard filled Silvia in. Christy was the fifteen-year-old daughter of Tama, Merry's sister. She had tried suicide twice before.

"We took her under our wings," said Big Eyes. "We tried to help her, but we failed." He dropped his head in his hands and began to weep.

Leonard detailed the horrors of an epidemic of youth suicides on reservations all over the country. "For us, Christy's the sixteenth in only six months. She had serious depression problems. At first, she was fine. A happy child. She was big sister to the younger ones. She'd read to them, take them for walks. Then at thirteen she took a dive. Got into drugs. Her father died of alcoholism. Her mother has depression too. They got it from being abused by the church boarding schools and from being Indian in this country. These kids lose hope." His voice rose higher when he said, "They don't see anything good in their future. But Christy – " Tears were rolling down his face. "She lost her way."

Silvia's stomach clenched. The Lakota belief that every child was a sacred soul amplified their grief. Their heartbreak overwhelmed her with sadness, then with rage. Why hadn't the mainstream newspapers and TV reported such a catastrophic story?

When the traditional mourning period ended, Dakotah's team agreed it was essential to honor Christy's life by finding ways to diminish the suicide epidemic. Dakotah called for a vision quest to reach for the highest possible inspiration. They would use the vehicle of a sweat lodge.

Silvia was eager to take part. She had experienced a sweat lodge on a reservation near D.C. and liked the way it purified, like a steamy sauna, and exposed some bad attitudes she needed to purge.

It was early morning when the team members, plus Merry, entered the lodge the men had made by stretching canvas over bent young tree branches. Dakotah began the ceremony with drum beating while Maya poured water on red-hot rocks that had been heated earlier. As the temperature rose, Silvia felt the wet steam opening her senses and releasing tension from places she didn't realize were tense. Even her face muscles relaxed.

When it was time to pass the talking stick, she listened as some shared what the Creator had told them in dreams, some gave prayers and others spoke of problems that bothered them. When Silvia's turn came, she spontaneously sobbed out her torment about the divorce and separation from the kids. She prayed the family could come together again.

During the final round, Silvia knew she had to speak about why she was there. Her hands trembled when she took the talking stick. Here she was, about to give spiritual advice to listeners whose spiritual depth was so much greater than her own. Her voice quivered.

"The Divine Mother said the time has come for Native Americans to learn how to use the power the Creator gifted you at birth. You can learn to balance and heal yourselves and your people. She said when you are healed, you will help non-native people connect to their power so they will respect Mother Earth and all the people that abide on her." Silvia's final words were almost whispered. "She – um – she sent me to teach you what I've learned from her."

The next morning the team met around the conference table. Dakotah's face was glowing. "We all look bright-eyed and bushy-tailed this morning. The sweat lodge brought us closer, cleared away some internal debris. At least we know we're the same species."

"Yeah, but what species?" Leonard grinned mischievously. "You must be thinking squirrels, but I'd rather we be foxes. Hairy-tailed. Not bushy."

"We'd be better off as thin-tailed tigers. Something we can ride swiftly over mountains while we track and kill evil." Maya joined the fun.

Everyone spoke at once, joking about their animal preferences. Dakotah spoke loudly and got back the attention. "So . . . on this journey coming up, we'll need to be snake-like sometimes, sometimes like eagles, sometimes like cougars. We'll do what the Creator guides us to do. But today I suggest we begin with whatever

Silvia needs to tell us." Dakotah caught the eye of everyone around the table. "I'm ready."

Everyone agreed.

Silvia was ready too. She led them outside to sit in a circle on the ground – "to be closer to Mother Earth". She was amazed at the strength of the collective vibrations when she guided them through the awakening. Clearly they already had many strands of kundalini active. Everyone beamed and Silvia knew they felt the joy.

"Okay. So this power isn't new to you, but you don't know how to raise it up at any time and diagnose which plexus, organs, nerves, and brain sections need attention."

Everyone still had their eyes closed, reluctant to come out of the bliss. Finally Dakotah opened his eyes and spoke tenderly. "We want to know everything."

Silvia explained how the body's spiritual complex aligns with the three main channels of the central nervous system. "The left carries the emotions, desires and thoughts about the past. The right carries the physical actions and thoughts about the future. The central channel – parasympathetic – integrates the two. When our left and right sides are balanced, our attention can rest in the center. In the present time. In reality."

Silvia demonstrated how to restore balance after veering too far left with symptoms of depression or negative thoughts about themselves. "On the opposite side, the right side, if you're too hyper, too much thinking that you can't stop, or you can't get to sleep easily, or are constipated; it means you have too much heat in your right side." She showed them the simple way the Divine Mother gave to remove the heat.

When the session ended, Merry spoke slowly, her voice thick with warmth. "It takes a mother to save mankind. Who else, but a mother – a Divine Mother – would create a method simple enough for all of us to do it ourselves? No middleman. No hierarchy." She put her hand on her heart and bowed her head. "The Divine Mother *is* a sacred teacher – a White Buffalo Calf Woman."

Basking in the glow of success as a coach, Silvia felt a familiar tug on the left side of her temple. Ah ha! Mister ego poked up his ugly head. She quickly smacked it down, glad to have captured the bloke before self-aggrandizement took over. After all, she was not the source of the knowledge. She felt blessed to be able to pass on such a precious gift so easily.

A few days later, Merry told Silvia she wanted to write a news story to tell the world about the Divine Mother's teachings; at least the part of the world covered by the *Big City Courier*. She asked Silvia to go with her to pitch the idea to her editor. "He'll be much more receptive if he sees that a white woman is also a believer."

Ed Perkins was a sixty year old white man who'd been on the job for several decades and lived in the same city his entire life. The women sat across from him at his desk that was strewn with files, newspapers and a huge ashtray filled with foul-smelling cigarette butts.

"Ed, I want to do a story about a new phenomenon; a discovery about the life force. It could be a good news piece, one that affects every person's mind, body, and soul."

Ed sat with his chin resting on his folded hands, elbows on the desk. He rolled his eyes. "Really? You mean supernatural stuff? Sounds flaky." He leaned back in his chair; slightly exasperated.

"No, I mean the physical life force inside of us. Not imaginary. It's a natural thing, like breathing. It's about the power of spiritual energy and how to use it to heal ourselves."

Ed, obviously annoyed, shook his head. But before he could say anything, Silvia smiled and spoke to his reaction. "The trouble is a lot of us think the spiritual realm is a scary mystery. Is that your take?"

"Yes. Hocus-pocus. It's a realm that is better to stay away from. Witches and all that."

Silvia's shoulders shrank. He sounded just like Charlie. She knew he wouldn't touch this story with a ten foot pole.

Merry persevered. "It's about a spiritual connection indigenous people have that most non-indigenous folks don't. Come on, let me tell the story about it. Then you'll learn too."

"Uh-oh, now you sound racist. See, here's the problem. If we publish a story about some weirdo new religion, which is what this sounds like, every other flaky religious fanatic will come out of the walls and want the same treatment. Believe me. This is America. There are a lot of them out there and they all cry theirs is the truth and want access to the press. The answer is no. Write a story about the girls' high school basketball team. We could use an update on them."

Merry gently pushed the office door shut. Ed put his hands over his eyes and groaned. "Oh, geez. Now I'm gonna get the big pitch."

"Yes, you are," Merry said. The firmness in her voice was clear. "This story needs to get out there. If you prefer, I could do it in the form of a profile of a great teacher. An Asian woman who Mahatma Gandhi sought counseling from about how to meditate – when she was just a child."

"Oh, that does it, an Indian guru. No dice. Do you know how many of those bearded, glassy-eyed shysters are in the U.S. now, collecting fortunes from starry-eyed seekers? No way. No way. The answer is no. That's my final no."

Silvia looked at Ed and shook her head. "Granted there are a lot of fakers out there. But what about the real ones, like Jesus? Do you really want to turn thumbs down to the scoop of the century?"

Ed stood to end the meeting. "Yes. Sorry, ladies. Come back if someone walks on water or is resurrected from death. Then you'll get a green light."

In the Project Place conference room, Maya was the first to present a proposal to deal with the suicide epidemic. "It seems to me we've been handed the way to help young people run away from the dark forces. The Divine Mother's program is awesome. Already I can feel the difference. I'm beginning to know how strong we are with the power we have and have always had. A few days ago, I started to get depressed and all I did was scoop the energy up outside my right sympathetic and push down my left until – *whammo* – the depression was gone! What could be simpler? We gotta get this program out there to the young people pronto."

She took some folded papers – notes – out of her jeans pocket, studied them for a few seconds, then tossed them in the trash. "I was gonna give one of those corporate-type presentations – you know, step 1, step 2 – but never mind trying to be complicated. This isn't."

She told them it was urgent to get the meditation into the schools, every school, right away. "And sessions should be given at least three times a week, pairing meditation with treatment. And attendance should be mandatory even if the kids just sit and don't participate. They can't be forced to partake, but the reluctant ones will benefit from the group's energy just by being there."

Maya said that another target group would be the parents, relatives, counselors and youth-group leaders.

"We can let the kids who catch on become teachers to help us do this. And we can integrate the Divine Mother's program with all the other efforts underway to prevent suicide."

"Aókiyapi," Dakotah said.

"Aókiyapi," Leonard said.

Big Eyes, Morten and Sariah all repeated the word.

Silvia nodded and smiled. "So what does it mean?"

Dakotah gave a poetic translation. "I'm in harmony with what you say."

For a month, Silvia worked with the team to introduce the program to the reservation's school board members, teachers and officials. Most of them instantly felt the realization and understood its value, a fact that Silvia concluded was due to their Native American DNA. In her other world, most reacted like Ed Perkins.

By fall, when the school term began, not only did they have full permission to offer the meditation program, but a free breakfast for each child was provided to sweeten the requirement for mandatory attendance.

To see for herself how the students reacted, Silvia visited a class led by Suni, a forty-year-old teacher, wife and mother. Eighth-grade boys and girls sat on the floor in a circle. A few of them giggled, which the teacher ignored.

"Let's close our eyes and keep our attention on top of our heads while we listen to music." Suni's voice was soft and soothing.

The snickering stopped when the room filled with sounds of a flute trilling through steady drum beats. Silvia joined in meditation but opened her eyes after ten minutes to see how many of the kids were actually in mental silence.

She did not expect to see what she saw. All eyes were closed and bodies relaxed.

Fifteen minutes later, the music faded and the group was asked to slowly open their eyes. "Now, let's see how we feel. Joey?" Suni nodded toward a boy who looked sleepy. "You said you had a headache when we sat down."

"It's gone." He smiled.

"What about you, Peta?"

"I was hyped-up when we first started. Now I'm cool." His tone was matter-of-fact.

One of the girls spoke. "I felt crappy. My mom and I had a gigantic fight last night. Now I don't feel mad at her anymore."

"Tahatan, how about you?"

He blushed. "With the music, well . . . it was okay."

The bell rang. The students collected their book-bags and hurried out.

Silvia glowed. "I'm amazed. At their age, struggling with puberty and all. They do this and do it so well! What makes it work?"

"One thing is they want the free breakfast and they don't get it unless they agree to sit with us afterwards. Even the ones who hate the idea have to join the circle, but we don't try to make them meditate. I tell them to just listen to the music. So far, everyone, even if they have a bad attitude like Tahatan; they get swept in. And these kids are really into music. I ask them for suggestions about what to play. Is that a bad idea?"

"No, gosh no. Although I wouldn't think rock and roll would work, would it?" Silvia laughed.

"I do censor their suggestions. I mean, I don't say no, I just preview them. If it's too jumpy, I don't play them. The rule is the music has to be non-vocal, so no Elvis. So far, it's worked out."

Silvia asked about parents' reactions. "The ones who are involved with their kids called right away to get more details about the meditation. When I told them there was a nighttime program for them to find out for themselves, they were eager to attend. The parents who are on drugs get the kids to school on time so they can have the free breakfast. That's progress. And I tell the kids who have problem parents they help them just by meditating because they spread good vibes in their homes. Some kids get it, some don't."

Suni's soft eyes connected with Silvia's. "I can tell you, for me personally, it's been dramatic from the first time. I change for the better a little bit every day. I'm less grouchy; have more energy. My job's more like an adventure now, instead of the hopeless grind it was at least half the time. For me, this meditation is a miracle!"

Later that day, Silvia, alone in her bedroom, celebrated her good fortune. She was blessed to be invited into a community where love was the dominant force. To speak with anyone was soul to soul – close – not distant nor reserved. Her optimism soared. If the majority of Americans got connected to their spirit like most Natives and practiced meditation, racism would die of natural causes. Just like any other negativity, it would be obliterated when pressed up against the cleansing from the Almighty spirit.

Merry tapped on the door and said she had a phone call.

"Mother? How are you?" Silvia asked.

"Well, not so good. I've got some bad news." She cleared her throat.

Silvia heard nasal sounds; her mother had been crying.

"Your father was hit by a car on his morning run. I saw him in the hospital; he was totally crushed. And while his heart was still beating, he . . . You know he never wanted any life support. So . . . so after a while I told them to let him go."

Silvia's heart pounded, and she felt hot, then cold. Somehow she was elevated above grief. "How are *you* doing?"

"I'm okay. Dealing with the nonsense of them telling me they have to do an autopsy. I can't see why on earth? Everything in his body looked crushed. It was obvious how he died. But they're telling me it's the law here."

Her mother's annoyance informed Silvia she was her everyday practical self. Grief had not crippled her. "Have you called the others yet?"

"Only Charlotte. I'm going down the line."

"Do you want me to make some calls?"

"No. It's better if I do it. I can give the details and they can hear in my voice that I'm okay."

"Good. I'm coming as soon as I can get a flight. I'll call with the arrival time. Okay?"

"That's good."

"Mom, I love you."

"I love you too."

Silvia wondered why she wasn't crying. She found her housemates and told what had happened and that she would leave the next morning. "He was seventy years old and still jogged every morning. He always said he wanted to die with his boots on. Well, that's what he got." The quip caught in her throat. Merry and Dakotah immediately put their arms around her. Still, the tears didn't flow.

"I've got to book a plane ticket. Can you get me to the airport?"

"Of course" Dakotah said. "You make your plans and we'll make them happen."

11

On the flight to D.C. she remembered her father. Especially she was proud of his strong stance against racism and anti-Semitism. Like when she was age twelve he found out the ice skating club where she trained would not permit Jews or blacks to join. He immediately withdrew membership even though it ended her career hope to become a good enough figure-skater to join the *Ice Capades*. She realized now that it was remarkable that even though she was passionate about dancing on ice, she never regretted the loss. She was in total sync with his moral stance.

Her dad's personal friendships with blacks and Jews, who frequently came to dinner, was unusual for those times when bigoted real-estate laws kept them from being neighbors. And as head of a government department, her father hired blacks during an era when most of his colleagues would not.

But he did have some flaws. While his passion for helping others was a constant, it was only for those outside the home. Inside was another story. When faced with serious emotional upsets of an immediate family member, he'd hide – shrink away from the scene.

In those days she never tagged him a coward like she would for anyone else who hid from emotional problems. She always excused him as being like most men of his era; emotionally illiterate. Handicapped, yes, but never a coward. Now she saw her lack of objectivity about her hero-father.

When she arrived at the airport, Silvia felt like a celebrity when the kids smothered her with hugs and kisses. They talked excitedly while Aunt Charlotte drove them to Helen's house. The plan was to all stay together to keep the new widow surrounded by children and grandchildren until the worst had passed.

Over the next few days Silvia helped with funeral preparations and wondered where was her grief? Was she in denial that her dear father was gone? Even during the memorial service when she read a poem in celebration of his life, her voice over the microphone was steady and clear. But as she returned to her seat, she caught sight of the somber faces of the grandchildren he'd left behind. Their profound loss finally overwhelmed her. The tears flowed.

She stayed in the pew long after the service had ended. Her racking sobs had ebbed to drizzles when a pair of strong arms wrapped around her. She looked up, expecting to find her brother. Startled, she drew back. Her comforter was Frank!

"Surprised to see me?" He looked into her eyes. "You father was such a good man. I wanted to be here for your mother and you all."

Shivers tingled up her spine. "I'm so glad you came." She put her hand on his arm. Sometimes terrible family tragedies bring tremendous blessings.

Silvia stayed to help her mother through the aftermath; not only to give comfort, but to take care of the insurance, banking and other paperwork that accompanies death. Her father's after-my-death checklist, complete with notations about document locations, made the job easy.

When the work was done, Silvia phoned Marilyn. They talked for hours, catching up on everyone's lives. Marilyn was designated leader of the public meditation at the library the next evening, so of course, Silvia would attend. She never missed an opportunity to meditate with a group of people, even if they were beginners. The synergy accelerated the vibrations in the room, soothing tensions to a much greater degree than when meditating alone.

Marilyn had begun the introduction when Silvia arrived so she quietly slipped into the back row. She scanned the room to see how many had come. A familiar shape was sitting in the front row. Frank! A burst of adrenaline flooded her body.

Her heart beat sped up like a race runner. What if he actually got it? God, if the meditation worked for him, the children would do it too. What more could a mother want?

She sucked in her breath when Marilyn asked if anyone felt deeply relaxed, or detected a cool breeze over their head. Frank's hand went up. Oh God, yes! Yes! Her fingers cupped her mouth to smother a gasp.

To hide her schoolgirl excitement, she held back from approaching him. He probably didn't even know she was there. When he finally stood and looked in her direction, she nodded and meandered to his side.

"So?" she asked.

Frank smiled. Then he blushed and looked toward the floor. "I have to admit, this is something. *Really* something!" He looked directly into her eyes. "I've never felt so . . . so . . . Oh, what's the word? Peaceful." He put a hand on his stomach. "So relaxed in here."

Silvia abandoned her aloof façade and squeezed his arm. "I know exactly what you mean. I had the same reaction first time. And it only gets better and better."

For a few moments they enjoyed a pulsating silence.

"Hey, are you busy now? Want to come and have a beer with me?"

Silvia wasn't about to tell him she didn't drink beer anymore. "I'd love to!"

Marilyn stood close by and heard their conversation. She caught Silvia's eye, smiled, mouthed 'have fun' and gestured goodbye; a graceful dismissal of their plans to have coffee together after the program.

As Frank turned the car into a familiar street, he grinned at her. Silvia laughed. "Okay. So, do I have to guess where we're going?"

"Yes."

"Hmm . . . okay. There's only one place to get a beer on this road, but it's expensive."

"True, but it's steeped in history. Teddy Roosevelt hung out where we're going and then so did we. We have a history at this place."

"Yeah," Silvia said. "I remember going outside to look at the stars. Two drunkards climbing up on the rocks."

"But we were wise enough to stay until we could climb down without breaking our necks," said Frank. "Happy memories."

At the tavern, when the waitress asked them what they were drinking, Silvia deferred to Frank.

"A Budweiser, please. The same for you?"

"Actually, I feel like a Coke."

Frank gave her a long look. "You're not drinking beer?"

"Not so much. It messes up my real high." She sucked in her breath and hoped her truthfulness would be well taken.

"Oh yeah?" He didn't pursue her words but leaned back in the booth. "I have to be honest with you. I didn't expect to get anything out of the meditation but confirmation that this thing you were into was crazy."

"Oh?"

"Yes. But to my surprise, it's not a flaky, leap of faith thing; it's physical, tangible. I could feel it move around inside and coolness coming out here." He put his palm above his head. "But the main thing was the way it relaxed me, like a tranquilizer." He gently patted his heart.

Silvia nodded. "I know. It was the same for me first time. So, congratulations." She reached for his hand and gave it a squeeze. "Now you are a realized soul."

Frank laughed and kept his hand in hers. "Realized? Me? What do I realize?"

"All your senses will gradually open up – sight, taste, hearing, smell and best of all, joy. You'll realize how much better life is when your spirit is your commander-in-chief. No more pendulum swing back and forth; happy or sad, hyper or lazy. You'll get balanced. It's like when you were a little kid – you woke up happy every morning and stayed in the present moment all day."

Within the mellow ambience of music and soft lights, they talked about the children's triumphs and tragedies and some facets of their lives after separation. Their light, cheerful attitudes eased the way in and out of what could have been an emotional disaster when they shared their romantic relationships. Frank and

Kate dated for about the same six months as Silvia and Charlie. Frank said their break-up was primarily due to her disinterest in children. Both felt fortunate they hadn't entangled the kids in their love affairs.

Eventually they wandered outside, climbed the rocks and watched the stars. With their heightened awareness, they championed the brilliance emanating from billions of galaxies and acknowledged the smallness of their place in the universe. Then they laughed at their aged profundity compared to their silliness when they were courting on these rocks eons ago.

The drive home began in silence. Silvia stared out the side window, steeped in memories of their time together before marriage. They often came to the same inn for beers and stayed in the parking lot smooching until her need to get home before curfew cooled them down. She was deeply in love. Not just because he was a football and basketball star, although in high school and college these features mattered. Mainly her heart was captured by his subtle sense of humor and kind, honest nature. She remembered the emotions and turned to look at him.

Frank returned the look for a second and grinned. "What are you thinking about?"

Silvia laughed. "I'm not telling."

"Okay." He laughed too, glanced at her then back to the road. "I'll tell you what *I* was thinking."

"Okay. Good." She was relieved he didn't prod her.

"Remember the time we drove to Detroit in my '41 Chevy to see the Lion's play the Baltimore Colts? And those cops stopped us for driving under the minimum speed? God, how we laughed about it being illegal to drive less than forty miles an hour."

"Yes, and you said they should have given you a medal instead of a ticket for driving the oldest car in Detroit."

"Bet you don't remember who won the game."

"Are you kidding? How could I forget. We were the only ones in the stands rooting for Baltimore. I remember the seriously angry faces of those Detroit fans when we won in the last three minutes. We were lucky to get out of there alive."

They chatted happily down memory lane until they reached Helen's house. Frank got out of the car, walked around and opened Silvia's door. She was glad she didn't forget his gentlemanly ways and leap out before his gesture. He walked her to the front door, planted a kiss on her forehead and without another word, waved goodbye as he drove away.

The next morning, Silvia and her mother sat together at breakfast. Gleaming sun rays deposed any darkness that lingered from their grief and filled the room with restorative grace. Silvia scanned her mother's face for signs of distress, but saw none. Her mother was a strong and practical woman. She wasn't one of those older people afraid to face death. She said it was perfectly clear that people died, so the thing to do was to make sure relationships were in order and material possessions downsized to the bare minimum. Silvia reminded her that she had a bit of downsizing to do before she could plan to depart this world. Helen had a large collection of copper, brass and mosaics from her travels to the middle and far East. Travels that Silvia and her siblings were sorry to have been denied, as their parents didn't enter the foreign service until their own kids were married and tied down with their families and careers.

During their quiet conversation, Helen took Silvia's hand and pulled it to her heart. "I know I've said this over and over, but it's meant so much to me that you did all this work, took care of the paperwork. You gave me such a – a – well, it's a gift. Now I don't have to spend all those hours on the phone and drive around dropping off death certificates."

"Mom, please. It gave me an excuse to stay with you longer and spend more time with the kids." They hugged each other tightly.

"When do you plan to go back to the reservation?"

"I talked to Dakotah late last night, and he asked me to come back as soon it felt right cause the demand for classes was growing and he needed more workers. That's great news."

Silvia gazed out the window as the thought crossed her mind that she'd like to stay long enough to see what Frank had in mind for them, if anything.

"What are you thinking about, dear?"

Silvia jerked out of her musing. "What do you mean?"

"Come on, a mother knows. We may have lived apart for a long time, but I'm still your mother, and I know there's something going on with you."

"Well, I meditate all the time now. It makes a difference. I'm pretty happy most of the time."

"That's not what I'm talking about. I've been with you enough since you got involved in meditation. I've seen the changes in you. You're much nicer, I have to say. But something's changed since the funeral. What's going on?" She clasped Silvia's hands, and her expression said she would not back off until she got an answer.

Silvia's face heated, embarrassed to even think about what was going on, let alone talk about it. "Well, okay. It's Frank." She smiled broadly.

"I knew it! I knew it the minute I saw him at the funeral." She clapped her hands happily.

"Nothing's happened. Well, yes it has in a very important way. He came to the meditation class and really liked it. God, I can't believe I'm saying this." She stood and paced around the kitchen island. "Afterwards we went out to one of our old haunts, back from when we were dating. We had a really nice time. That's all."

Her mother threw back her head and flung her hands into the air. "I knew it! If only your father could be here now. He'd really love it if your family got back together." She angled her head to look out at the sky through the kitchen window. "Well, maybe he is helping orchestrate this whole thing." Helen's eyes glazed over.

Before her mother could get weepy, Silvia joked. "No doubt he's up there telling God how to get better organized." Helen brightened so Silvia quickly changed the subject. "Shall we make lunch for the children here or do you feel like going out to a restaurant?"

During her time on the reservation, Silvia kept in close touch with the Unity House crew, so knew about the big changes. John and the board had accepted a government grant to merge Unity House with a group of black professionals who focused on the future cable television industry – the technology that would soon replace over-the-air broadcasting. The mission was to develop business opportunities for blacks in early days of the industry's start-up. Like everyone else who cared about economic growth for blacks, Silvia applauded the concept. After all, the new company could create solid careers in engineering, equipment manufacturing and even cable business ownership. Yet she couldn't help the sadness she felt over the loss of their intimate, highly energized, flexible little group that could change direction in a flash when an opportunity arose. This was no merger; it was the death of Unity House.

Silvia expected to find her colleagues in a similar state of sorrow when she visited them before returning to the reservation. Instead she found Lisa cheerfully packing boxes while *Rhythm & Blues* blared out over the radio. Brad wasn't there as he took the week off before their move. And John was eager to take her to see the new offices.

Silvia made a pouty face. "Am I the only one that's feeling sad about leaving our beautiful, unbureaucratic Unity House?"

"Oh, we've already been through that; we mourned for a few days." John said. He put his arm around Silvia's shoulder and gave her a squeeze. "Come on, you'll be fine when you see the new digs."

"Yes you will," said Lisa. She smiled knowingly.

Silvia froze when the elevator doors opened on the seventh floor of the glass and marble building. "Oh my God!" Her first sight was an exquisite bouquet of fresh, yellow roses nestled in a gorgeous jade vase, posed on a highly polished mahogany and glass reception desk. John lead her down a long beige carpeted corridor of spacious glass enclosed offices, past several conference rooms, a library, a copy machine room and into a small kitchen. They sat at a round table and drank fresh coffee while John showed her the directory of department heads and staff members who were already on the job. Silvia noticed that all the people she saw wore formal business attire. "I see the dress code we had at Unity House has been seriously upgraded." said Silvia. "When can I meet these folks?"

"Sorry, not today. I've got a meeting back at Unity House in twenty minutes. You'll get to know everybody as soon as you're ready to join us. When are you coming back for good?"

"My best guess is after Christmas. Will I still have a job?"

"Are you kidding? You're one of the few people that can type. You'll always have a job."

Silvia playfully smacked him on his shoulder. "Male chauvinist pig."

John threw his head back and laughed. "That reminds me of a joke. What's worse than a male chauvinist pig?"

Silvia shrugged.

"A woman who won't do what she's told."

Silvia snickered. She felt giddy, yet at the same time, grateful. How blessed can one be? A relevant job surrounded by good people. She flashed a warm smile and held her eyes on John's. "So, Unity House didn't die after all. It just transformed – from a small fish into a whale."

John chuckled. "I hope we make big waves and not just a lot of blubber. This work won't be easy. The communication giants we have to deal with are not likely to let us in gracefully. Rumor has it they don't like to share."

12

After only three weeks away from the reservation, Silvia was amazed that ten schools out of the total eighteen had the meditation program going regularly. Dakotah explained. "It only takes a few sessions before the teachers are comfortable as meditation leaders. Just like us – most of them take to it immediately."

Silvia asked how they were dealing with the folks strung out on drugs and alcohol, since so many tribal members were addicted.

"It's part hopeful, part hopeless," Dakotah said. "The ones in treatment are being offered meditation as one of their options. Their counselors love it, but it's too soon to tell how well it will work over the long haul. As for the real down and outers, they're the tough ones, like hard rocks. Maybe – but it's a big maybe – if they get into treatment, we can make progress." He suggested she go see the toughest cases for herself.

Silvia borrowed a car and drove to the town that housed the beer and liquor stores. Located a few yards beyond the reservation border, the town held a monopoly on booze since the tribal government had for decades banned liquor sales on its property. The town's population of only ten residents enjoyed a financial bonanza. Every year they sold over four million cans of beer to residents of the nearby reservations.

The moment she hit town, a tragic sight panged her stomach with nausea and filled her eyes with tears. Out in the open, on the concrete steps outside a cluster of small liquor stores, lay dozens of drunken men and women. Despite the chilly fall air, they were clothed only in T-shirts and jeans, no coats or blankets in sight.

Silvia approached a woman who looked awake and sat down beside her on the steps. Her red eyes were open, though her stare was vacant. Her breath was raspy.

"Hello." Silvia touched the woman's limp arm to share some of her own energy in hopes the woman felt the warmth. "My name's Silvia; what's yours?"

"Name's Yella-Fetah." She slurred her words.

"Yellow Feather?"

She nodded.

"You live on the rez?"

With an annoyed sigh, Yellow Feather slowly pulled herself to a sitting position.

Compassion filled Silvia's heart. "I'm a friend. I'd be happy to drive you home or wherever you'd like to go."

"Wha? I don't wanna go nowhere. Here's where I wanna be. I'll need a drink soon." She spoke defiantly, but her tone changed when she said, "You wanna buy me a six-pack?" Then, having exhausted her energy, Yellow Feather slumped back down onto her concrete bed.

Silvia approached a couple who had moved to an upright position when they saw her.

"Hi, I'm Silvia. I'm staying nearby. Did you all walk here from the rez? Can I give you a ride home?"

The couple looked to be about fifty and it was clear they had binged for a long time. Their hair was streaked with mucus and dirt. Their red eyes were swollen; their clothes filthy.

"Wha? Don't ya see my Cadillac over there just waiting for us?" The man had a surly grin as he waved his arm weakly toward the street. No car was in sight.

Silvia went along with his fantasy. "Oh yeah, but the tires are flat and it has no gas."

The man looked confused. The woman cackled, "Why don't ya just sit on down and have a drink wif us. You buyin'?"

"Nope, just passing by. I'll drive anybody back to the rez who wants a ride." She looked around at the other lost souls passed out on the sidewalk. At this stage of their addiction, they did not want to be rescued. Silvia was told they would hang around until their money ran out, then drag their tortured bodies back to their shacks until the next subsidy check arrived.

Driving back to Project Place, Silvia contemplated the huge power alcohol had over not just these extreme cases, but she herself had been trapped in the social drinking myth. Before ending her relationship with alcohol, she wondered what in the world she would do if she did not drink when she got together socially with friends. After she and alcohol 'divorced', she found out no matter the beverages, parties were always fun.

Now she had to agree with Dakotah that if these *down and outers* didn't get into treatment, the alcohol's poison would win the battle for their souls.

"There's a letter for you." Merry smiled with her head cocked and eyebrows raised.

"Why are you looking like that? From one of my kids?"

"Nope, the return clearly says Frank Nolan Sr. I couldn't help seeing it."

Silvia's cheeks flushed as she tore the envelope open on the way to her room.

Dear Silvia: I apologize for thinking you were into some type of witchcraft when I heard you were enamored by some spiritual thing. It's embarrassing to find oneself to have been so prejudiced. Now that I'm doing that same spiritual thing, I've found what's happening to me almost too good to be true. It's just like you said it would be — joy most of the time like when I was a kid. Yesterday, when my boss came at me with his usual pressure to churn out a report faster, I didn't react, not even in my gut. Just smiled and told him I understood his frustration. At first he looked at me like I was an alien. Then he smiled and walked away. It was obvious he'd been disarmed.

I wouldn't want to have to miss the group mediation. There's usually about fifteen of us and I can feel the vibrations pretty well. I don't feel as much when I meditate at home by myself. But when I skip it, I don't feel as good. I keep wishing you were here so I could find out everything you know about this way of life. I would call you, but as you know, I'm not a good talker. Writing gives me the time I need to find the words.

I haven't involved the kids in this yet. Thought I'd get better at it first. Frankie's too old to just do as I do anymore; he questions everything, as you well know. Wish there was a program for kids. Is there something going on for their ages?

Please write back.

Love, Frank

Dear Frank: I'm thrilled the meditation works for you! It's a great idea to have programs for kids – we can put one together when I get back.

How is your mother reacting to you as a meditator?

The suicide prevention program I told you about has caught on like wildfire. I'm not surprised though, since most natives were born realized. All they need now is to learn the healing treatments. I'm ecstatic about how quickly they embrace the whole thing. What a difference between them and non-natives. What to do to wake up more of our people?

Must get this to the post office before the last pickup, which happens only a few times a week in this remote part of the world. But then, I do love the remoteness. Nature is so vast it never lets you forget that it's there. Especially the sky – have never experienced so much sky – more of it touches the ground yet more of it goes into eternity. Awesome!

Give hugs and kisses to the kids and ask them to send letters and pictures.

Love, Silvia

One evening after dinner, she went for a walk with Leonard and Big Eyes. Their way was lighted by a full moon and billions of stars clear to the eyes without the blur from city lights. They followed a path that led to the local college where they saw the shadowy outlines of a group of small boys on picnic tables, bouncing around as boys do. When they spotted adults heading toward them, the boys jumped on ponies haltered nearby. Galloping at full speed, they howled furiously as they bore down on the startled threesome.

"Duck! Protect your head!" Big Eyes shouted.

When the horde reached their targets, one boy slowed his horse, leaned down, and tried to grab Silvia. He was small, so she easily broke his hold with her fist.

The boy held his seat and circled back to join his buddies who had stopped to watch from a distance.

"They're gonna regroup and come back," Big Eyes warned. "This time, Leonard, you and I will pull a couple off their horses. Silvia, you just stay crouched with your back to them. Indian ponies are too smart to trample down a person."

When the swarm of howling youngsters returned, this time they wielded base ball bats. Leonard and Big Eyes easily grabbed their weapons and yanked two boys from their horses, letting them hit the ground hard. Silvia crouched for a moment, but then rose up and pulled another boy off his horse. Now the adults held three captives. The remaining four rode off again to a safe distance, then turned to watch what would happen next.

Big Eyes gruffly stared at the captives. It was clear they were young – nine or ten at the most. "You and your buddies made a big mistake coming after us, you know that? Huh?" He shook the shoulders of the boy in his grip, who looked away from the piercing eyes.

"We can have all of you put in jail and throw away the keys," Leonard said.

The boys tried to look defiant while Big Eyes tied their hands together with a rope that hung on the side of one of the saddles. With the three tied in a row, Leonard marched them toward the remaining group of wannabe hoodlums and shouted, "Throw down your bats and get off those horses."

The hefty size and gruffness of the men frightened the boys. They slid off their mounts and dropped their bats on the ground. As Leonard tied the other boys' hands, a few tried to break the hold. Their attempts only tightened the slip knots further, causing the boys to howl.

"What are you, wannabe Lakota warriors?" Big Eyes played the role of interrogator. He jerked the rope downward, forcing the group to the ground.

The boys all looked down. None spoke.

"Lakota warriors have honor. They would never attack their uncles and aunties. Maybe you're not Lakota. Maybe just a pack of coyotes in disguise." Big Eyes looked menacing with his hands on his hips.

"She's not our auntie. She's white," said one of the boys in disgust.

"Oh, I see. You're a Lakota warrior acting like some racist white person. Like the ones that believe all Indians are savages."

The boys looked down again.

Big Eyes turned to Leonard and Silvia. "Let's take them to the jailhouse and work them over."

"Good idea," Leonard said. He narrowed his eyes and slapped the rope end in his hand like a whip.

Silvia tried to look mean but had to bite her lips; the boys were so young their gangland imitations seemed almost comical. When they reached the house, she gave a halt signal to the men. "Let me tell the law enforcement officers inside the scum they have to deal with."

Dakotah and Merry welcomed the opportunity to mentor the would-be hoodlums and easily slid into their roles as prosecutors. They came outside and stood stiffly on the porch.

"Oh, it's Robin Feathers and Timber Richards. I know your relatives," said Merry. Her face was stoic; her tone threatened. As an active member of the community and a news reporter for many years, she knew most of the reservation families.

Dakotah took over as lead interrogator. "So you've been charged with intent to commit violent acts of warfare against your aunties and uncles. How do you plead, guilty or not guilty?"

The boys looked stunned and remained silent.

"Did you ride your ponies down upon these three adults, tried to swat them with your baseball bats? Yes or no?"

Robin Feathers spoke haltingly. "They made me do it."

"Who's they?" Dakotah asked.

"These guys. I didn't wanna. They said I acted like a girl." Fear made his voice pitch go higher. The other boys screwed up their faces in disgust.

Dakotah maintained his stern look and turned to Merry. "How many of these boys have brothers or cousins in gangs?"

"At least three of them that I know of."

He looked at the adults. "All right. What do you say we take on an anti-gang program for these particular hoodlums?"

No one hesitated; they all nodded.

"Leonard, would you guard the prisoners while we go work out their jail sentence?"

Silvia wavered between smiles and sighs as they made their way to the project workroom. There the team quickly put together a seven day a week mentoring program that included crafts, basketball and field trips. "It's like suddenly having a young family again," Merry said. "I always wanted more children and here they are."

Silvia was deeply moved by the time commitment her teammates made so instantly to a program that they agreed would require at least one year to steer the boys away from the desire to join gangs. No one she knew in her other world would take on such responsibility so quickly and happily.

The joy and smiles of the judicial team were erased when they returned to face their prisoners. Dakotah delivered the sentence.

"Tonight we will take each of you home and talk to your parents or guardians. We'll tell them what you've done and what's expected of you now. Then here's what you will do every day until we, your prison family, say your term is over.

"Your daily schedule includes you being at school at 7 a.m. for the free breakfast and meditation session. If you're ever a no-show, ten days will be added to your sentence of already three hundred and sixty-five days. That's a one-year jail term." He grinned. "And that's ten additional days for each offense."

The boys sat stiffly, their eyes wide, their lips clenched tight.

"After school you will come directly to the jailhouse and do your school homework under supervision by the jailhouse personnel. After dinner you will be escorted back to your homes. On the weekends, you will stay at the jailhouse full time. That's every Saturday and Sunday you will sleep, eat, and do what we tell you to do."

Silvia and Merry teamed up to take Robin and Timber home. Robin's elder sister, Cindy Lou, invited them in. "Is Quanta here?" Merry asked. She knew Robin's mother.

"She's out for the night; I'm in charge." Cindy Lou looked pained. "She fell off the wagon again."

Silvia saw five other children, some older than Robin and two younger. The tiny bungalow was full of toys, clothes, empty soda cans and trash strewn everywhere. The children crowded around to see what was going on.

Merry took over as the senior adult. "Now you kids go on about your business. Robin, you go do your homework with the others and stay out of the kitchen. We're going there to talk."

Cindy Lou told them she won a scholarship to Black Hills University. Now she has to be surrogate mother to three younger siblings and three cousins whose parents are in treatment programs for alcoholism and drug addiction. She hopes at least one of the parents will be clean enough to take over so she can go to school next semester.

Merry read Cincy Lou into the details of Robin's misdeeds and told her the plan to mentor the boys away from gangs. Cindy was thrilled. "Robin worries me a lot. He's so willing to do whatever an older kid tells him to do, good or bad. One of his cousins is in the Wild Boyz, and they're always about recruiting. I can keep him safe for now, but what will happen when I go off to college?"

"Thank God for you!" Silvia said.

"And thank the Creator for you! I'm part of the meditation group and heard it was a white lady that had the visit from the White Buffalo Calf Woman. Is it you?"

Silvia shrugged and looked away.

Timber Richards' family was not as accommodating. When Silvia and Merry knocked, an older boy shouted for them to come in. He stayed sprawled on the couch smoking what smelled like marijuana. They found the other household members crowded around the kitchen table eating supper. The plates were piled high with spaghetti, with parmesan cheese sprinkled on top. No sauce. No meat. No vegetables.

"Where've you been?" Timber's father, Jake, spoke harshly to his son. Crow-dog, the grandfather, smiled at the women and signaled to the two girls at the table to get up and give their seats to the visitors. In a near whisper, the oldest girl asked if they'd like some food.

Merry squeezed the girl's hand. "Thanks, but no. We've come to bring Timber home and we need to talk to these two." She nodded in the direction of the men.

"All right, everyone go on out and shut the door behind you," Jake barked.

Earlier Merry told Silvia that Jake, as a recovering alcoholic was highly agitated much of the time so she planned to take a legal approach towards him. "Timber will be charged with attempted assault and battery if he does not participate in the mentoring program. But for it to work, you'll need to get him to school at seven every morning and to our house every Saturday morning, where he'll be incarcerated for the weekend."

She gave him time for reflection.

"And if I don't go along with this plan?"

"Timber will go to juvenile detention. And you know how that can hurt a boy his age."

"You should know, Jake. You were about Timber's age when I let them take you. After six months, you came back even meaner than when you went in," Crow-dog said.

"I was mad as hell at you! You could have kept me out, but no, you wanted me to learn some kind of lesson. That was thirty years ago, and it still pisses me off." He banged his fist down, rattling dishes on the table.

Silvia and Merry exchanged a silent look.

"Everything pisses you off. As the elder in the family, it's my duty to try to temper your nasty disposition." Grandfather's tone was even, without emotion. He was giving fact.

Jake slumped against the back of his chair. "Okay, we'll try it your way. Hey, maybe you could take on his brother too? He's a fifteen-year-old pothead. To keep that one out of gangland, we let him medicate himself and then we sit on him."

Silvia hoped Jake was joking. She knew how much Merry would want to help the older boy too. But there was a huge difference between small boy attitudes and big ones. She held her breath waiting for Merry's decision.

Merry shook her head. "Let's see how it works for the young ones first."

Silvia had kept mostly silent at the houses, but on the way home she poured out her distress. "God, they need bigger and better houses. It hurts my heart to see all those kids living like that. And in Timber's house there's no running water? They have to go outside to use the toilet? And in the winter? How do they even wash their clothes and brush their teeth? God, in this day and age; they have a TV but no toilets inside. This is tragic when some of us have umpteen bathrooms and swimming pools."

"Hey, take it easy, kiddo." Merry said. "When that's what you're used to, you don't spend much time in agony about using an outhouse. Didn't you ever sleep in a tent or someplace where you had to haul water from a pump and heat it on a stove?"

"I did. But only for an occasional weekend and always in the summer. When my kids were in diapers, I refused to go on camping trips." She wiped her arm across her forehead. "*Whoosh*, I am spoiled; a delicate darling."

A package of treasures arrived from Frank that included art work and school test papers from the children; the ones with good grades. In his letter, he spoke about his mother.

She likes what meditation is doing for me but isn't interested in trying it out for herself. She said she's like a dog; too old to learn new tricks.

Then he apologized again.

God, I did a lot of criticizing of you. Now I realize how much I hurt you, the children and myself by harboring all that anger."

Silvia read the letter again and again. In her reply she told the children she loved their drawings – yes, she'd hung them up. And she was proud of their splendid schoolwork. She sent some photos of their 'adopted' boys. To Frank, she wrote: *Don't beat yourself up. I put you through a horrendously difficult situation so I'd say we're pretty much even with the amount of hurt we heaped upon each other.*

The boys responded joyfully to the individual attention, solid meals, variety of activities and reliable structure to their 'prison' lives. They liked everything so much, they asked if they could stay over on the weekdays too. Dakotah said that this was the danger of giving them too many comforts compared to what they had in their own homes. He suggested they set up teepees in the backyard, cook outside and give up the TV.

"I like teepee living except it's starting to get cold," Leonard said. "We'll have to run power out there for my electric blanket."

"Oh yes and install a hot tub." Maya joined his farce.

Merry, being her sensible self, suggested that it would be good instead to help the boys appreciate the positive aspects of their own home life, like all the wonderful brothers and sisters they had to play with and help take care of.

"We could come up with work projects. Like cleaning up yards, doing some planting, stuff like that," Sariah said. "It works for my kids. I make them do chores even though they complain; louder now that they're teenagers. But deep down they thrive on having to do chores. Makes them feel useful. They learn it feels good to be givers, not just takers. It's the Lakota way of good parenting."

Silvia gleefully pounced on Sariah's last phrase. "You can't claim all the good ways of doing things. Many parents I know use that strategy. Actually, I think white people invented it."

"Oh yeah? Well, let's see, who was here first? Guess who you white people learned from?"

The women leapt to their feet, faking a wrestling match. Sariah scuffled the smaller, lighter Silvia to the ground, straddled her, and tickled her ribs. Extremely sensitive in that exact spot, Silvia laughed loudly and kicked her legs. The others crowded around, cheering them on. Merry stepped in to referee.

"All right, break it up, break it up. Shame on you both. Now we'll have to give you extra chores." She looked at the others. "What do you say we make these two cook our dinner?"

"I'll have steak and fried potatoes," Leonard said.

"Buffalo burger here," said Big Eyes.

"I'll have wajapi," Dakotah said. "In fact, we'll all have wajapi. So get busy." He waved the fighters into the kitchen.

"Wajapi?" Silvia whispered to Sariah. "Is that something edible?"

"It's fried bread, dummy. Our sacred food. Kept us alive when your ancestors took away our land. They paid for our millions of acres, rich with buffalo herds, deer, berries, nuts and grasses, with a few tiny bags of flour, salt and baking powder. Our people took those paltry crumbs and invented frybread – kept thousands of us from starving to death. Now we make it with dozens of variations; sweet, salty, with meat, vegetarian, whatever. We love it."

Silvia pondered for a moment. "You mean my ancestors stole your land and so they wouldn't feel guilty, pretended like they paid for it with a few bags of flour?"

Sariah put her hands on her hips. "Yep. Those are your people."

"Well, sorry, I can't do any cooking now. I'm too angry and depressed." Silvia faked a troubled face. "Can't put my terrible vibrations into the food. You'll have to do it all with your good energy."

Sariah hooted. "Oh no you don't. No way, foxy girl!" Sariah grabbed her arm. "You're not getting away with that!"

Silvia thought she was about to get smacked on the behind, when suddenly Sariah let her go and smiled sweetly. "I'll tell you what. You're gonna make the frybread. But you can do it as a sweet – with vanilla ice cream, dark chocolate syrup and whipped cream on the top. Will that bring back your happy vibes?"

Immediately Silvia's raised both hands up. Instant surrender.

The frequency of letters from Frank and the children increased. Frankie included a surprising revelation in one of his. *Before, Dad never talked about you, but now he does it all the time.*

She surmised this was to make amends for past behavior. But the fact that Frankie noticed what his dad was doing swelled her heart. Her little boy had reached a new level of maturity. What next? She shuddered at the realization that this sweet, some-what obedient child would soon become a teen-ager.

13

The "prisoner boys" continued to blossom in their tough-love environment. A field trip to a rodeo was planned to enrich their experiences and acknowledge their good behavior. The ride to the state fairgrounds was filled with excited chatter as the boys boasted about their rodeo knowledge.

"This bull my uncle told me about – Bushwacker – no cowboy ever stayed on him. Will Bushwacker be there?" Timber asked.

"I don't know, but he's a famous one. They say he snorts fire," Leonard said.

Throughout the hours of bronco busting, calf tying, clowning, barrel racing and finally the long-awaited bull riding, the boys jumped up and down with excitement. The adults were kept busy with trips for hot dogs, drinks, cotton candy and whatever it took to enhance the experience for the boys.

It was dark when the show ended so the group moved slowly through the parking lot towards their van. Each relived a different highlight as they chatted happily. Suddenly a barrage of cold liquid smashed into their faces. Shocked, and in pain, their hands flew to their eyes to remove the scum. Two white men with dripping buckets stood above them in the bed of a pickup truck, swaying with drunkenness and slurring epithets.

"Dirty Injuns. Go back to your reservation. We don't want you here!"

"Savages, get the hell out of here. You too, squaws. Filthy Injuns."

As their victims hurried past, one of the men pelted them with raw eggs and the other threw flour, covering the backs of their targets with a slimy mess.

Silvia, Merry and Maya instinctively huddled together, raising their arms into a protective shield over the boys. Leonard took charge. "Keep together, but move. Move quickly now! Let's get to the van."

Just as they were safely inside, a final threat rang out. "Red niggers! Whore squaws! Go on. Get out of our town! Git! Git! If you come back, you're dead!"

A rifle shot rang out as the pickup sped away.

"Crazy old sons-of-bitches. I'd like to – " Leonard cut himself off after a quick glance at the boys.

The women held the youngsters close, trying to soothe their fears. No one was crying, yet even the adults were badly shaken. All were wet from what smelled like beer, and raunchy from the eggs and flour.

"They were scary, acting like – like savages," Leonard said. His anger broke and his expression was near comical when he heard his own choice of words. "Yep, those old geezers, they're the ones who are filthy savages."

Robin raged, "Let's go fight 'em!"

"They have a rifle" Timber warned.

"That's not the way anyhow," Merry said. "Fighting is just what they'd like, so we'd be just as stupid as them."

Leonard was about to drive away when a white elderly woman tapped on his window. He cautiously rolled it down a few inches. She handed him a note.

"I'm Etta Jones. I saw what those devils did to you but couldn't do much to stop them. I got their license number, so you can have the police go after them." When she saw the frightened looks on the boys' faces, tears flooded her eyes. "My name and phone number are on there too, in case you need a witness." She quickly walked away before anyone could respond.

Back on the reservation, when the boys finally fell asleep, the traumatic tale was shared with Dakotah and Big Eyes, who had stayed behind.

"So overt racism in the city is still rampant?" Silvia asked.

Maya nodded. "I can never carry any bag, even my purse, inside the shops. The owners keep their eyes glued to me, certain I will steal something. They always inspect inside any bag any native carries."

"And on the bus some white people will get up and change their seat when a dirty injun like me sits next to him," Dakotah said.

"And what about being stopped by the police for no reason?" Leonard said. "They do it to me on a regular basis. They inspect inside my car and trunk in hopes they can arrest me for something."

"Are we going after those old geezers?" Silvia asked.

"We have a bunch of lawsuits charging racism in the works against various plaintiffs and the state," Dakotah said. "We could add these charges to the pile." His brow was furrowed, and a mix of pain and anger darkened his eyes. "But right now we have got to deal with the impact on the souls of our boys who are hated for being natives."

Silvia had a plan.

The next day was a bright Sunday morning. The boys and the adults sat on a rug that faced an altar decorated with lit candles and sage incense. Eyes were closed; energy was raised as the meditation had begun. Native flute music played softly in the background. Silvia's plan was underway.

"Let's put our right hand on our chest. This is where fear gets stuck like gum after we've been scared. Our kundalini vibrations are a hundred times stronger than the scared stuff. So, now we're going to blast away that yucky fear with the vibrations that flow out of our hand."

Several minutes passed and Silvia could feel on her finger tips that the sternum area was free from negativity. "The next place we need to clear out is in our foreheads. When we're mad at someone, our anger gets stuck here and blocks our energy flow. Let's put our hand on our forehead and silently say, not out loud, 'I forgive everyone for everything.' Say it ten times."

Robin protested. "I'm not forgiving those old geezers."

"*Your* anger blocks *your* brain; forgiveness clears it away. The bad guys don't care that you're mad at them. If you forgive them, doesn't mean they didn't do very bad things," said Dakotah.

The music continued during the meditation treatment until Silvia felt their foreheads were clear. She turned off the music.

"Now let's slowly open our eyes." She scrutinized the group and saw the relaxed faces, the shining eyes. "Okay. Put a hand over your head and if you feel coolness flowing out, nod."

All heads nodded.

"That cool breeze you feel, those are the vibrations. You can use them like a code. So let's take a test. I'm going to ask a question while you all hold your hands out like this." She held her palms facing upward. "Cool wind across your hands means yes; hot or nothing at all means no."

She waited until she saw all hands held palms open. "So here's the question: is it time to end this meditation?"

The boys felt their hands for a moment, then jumped up cheering. "It's cool! It's cool!" Everyone laughed.

"Can we go outside and shoot some hoops?" Timber asked.

Leonard grabbed the ball. "You can, but you have to get the ball away from your uncles." He raced outside, followed by all the males.

The women went into the kitchen to fix lunch. It dawned on Silvia that she never heard these women complain about housekeeping chores. In fact, the struggle for women's liberation wasn't apparent on the reservation – at least not the same way it was in her other world. Silvia felt respected by the men on the team *because* she was a woman. Later she asked Merry why women seemed to be more respected.

"It was the White Buffalo Calf Woman who gave sacred truths to us Lakotas that have been handed down as sacred knowledge over the years. Reverence for the spiritual and feminine qualities of women was one of those truths."

"I've got great news," Maya said as she chopped vegetables. "Cindy Lou told me her mother is meditating. Said Quanta had quit smoking and believed with the help of the Divine Mother, she soon wouldn't want to drink anymore."

"Tama told me some good stories too" Merry stopped shredding lettuce. "A few have thrown away their cigarettes. It's a miracle!"

Silvia didn't look up from her task of spreading mayonnaise on sandwich bread. "That's pretty quick," she said. "It took me six months to lose the desire to smoke."

"That's because you're of an inferior species," Maya quipped.

"Oh yeah? Well, you just blew your superior status with your big ego," Silvia said. She put down her knife and swatted Maya on the back of her head. "Now your ego is as big as mine."

"I have some bad news," Sariah put a chill on the banter. "Heard it just before coming here. A thirteen-year-old girl died yesterday. Suicide. Took a whole bottle of sleeping pills."

Everyone froze. Sadness invaded the women. "Oh God, from which school?" Silvia asked.

"Red Ridge High. Her name is Dancing Crow. Ninth grader. She'd been out sick with kidney problems for several months."

The women mulled over the news. Silvia's heart sank, her body wilted. It was the first suicide since their meditation program began.

Merry finally spoke. "Guess we've all been afraid to jinx our good luck by speaking out loud that there had been no suicides for months, a new record. But now . . ."

"I'll visit the school, help with the counseling," Maya said.

"I'll go with you," Sariah said. "We can join the morning meditations for a few days. Help the kids clear out their grief." She pounded on the table. "Damn, damn, damn!"

The women solemnly returned to their lunch preparations. Merry peeled cucumbers while she spoke. "I was so hoping we could win them all. We're probably all mulling the same thing. Maybe it was her sickness. Maybe she didn't attend the meditations. Maybe her parents kept her away. Maybe this, maybe that. But let's be realistic. We aren't going to win them all."

Silvia agreed. "But obviously *we* need to temper our expectations. We can't let our campaign lose its thunder."

Lunch making stopped. The native women looked at each other, then glared at Silvia. "Now see here, girl. Non-native girl." Maya gripped Silvia by the arms and spoke for the group as they circled around Silvia. "You accuse a Lakota woman of losing thunder? How'd you like to feel some lightening to go with our thunder?" She pressed her forehead against Silvia's; puckered her lips to keep a serious face. Silvia tried to look scared, but her laughter broke through.

"She has to be punished," said Sariah.

"Yes, let's torture her with a paddle wheel," said Maya.

The ladies stood in a row and made a bridge of legs. Silvia was ordered to get on her hands and knees and crawl through. She obeyed, but her giggles were louder than her fake howls of pain from the gentle spankings she got from each woman. The moment Silvia had crawled through the last pair of limbs, Dakotah came in, recognized the game, and expanded the bridge with his legs. "Don't know why Silvia's being punished, but am sure it's for a good cause. She didn't even feel the first pass through, so she needs to go through again."

At the threat of passing through the torture chamber again, Silvia jumped up and put her hands in the air. "I surrender and promise never again to say Lakota women are wimpy about anything."

Dakotah laughed. "You all are wimpy right now. The boys didn't just send me in to find out what all the hooting and hollering was about." He raised his voice loud enough for the boys to hear. "Where's our lunch?"

"You shout like that and you'll go through the paddle wheel next." Merry waved a finger at him. Dakotah covered his behind with his hands and hurried back outside.

Within ten minutes everyone was called in to savor the food and tell stories around tables put together to accommodate everyone. Silvia marveled at the high level of subtle bantering skill even the young boys had that enabled them to tease without hurting.

"Indian kids learn to dispense humor early on," said Big Eyes. "Laughter is good medicine."

14

Dear Silvia: In your last letter, when you told me you'd never lost your love for me, my spirit jumped for joy. My love for you never went away either and now it feels like my heart is wide open; a new thing for me.

What I'm about to ask you ought to be done in person. But since we still have some geography between us and I don't want to wait, please picture this. I'm on my knees, looking handsome with graying temples ('tho slightly bald), offering you a bouquet of your favorite yellow roses. Hear my humble request – will you remarry me?

Yours forever, Frank

Dearest Frank: Yes! Yes! Yes, I will!

Everlasting love, Silvia

P.S. The roses were great, and the graying temples made me swoon. You are so very handsome. But the real deal came when your proposal hit my heart. I'm also jumping for joy!

Back from the post office after Frank's response was sent special delivery, Silvia ditched her fear that she would jinx the reunion by premature leaks. Now her excitement would not be contained. "Guess what?" she said to her Lakota family who were crammed into the kitchen as they drank coffee and joked, native style.

"You got your red card so now you're legit on the rez?" Leonard asked.

"You have to renew every ten years, you know," Big Eyes added.

"That's a load off," Merry said. "Now we can quit paying her under the table."

Dakotah nodded. "And now you're no longer undocumented."

"Congratulations! You're the first white person to be granted amnesty," Maya said.

Silvia's body stiffened, her forehead wrinkled. The Lakota nation had immigration laws? She had undocumented friends who were illegal – always a little nervous and looking out for the law since they had overstayed their student visas. The look of concern on her face caused everyone to break into applause.

"We got you good this time," Merry said.

"Oh my God!" Silvia put her hand on her chest. "I can't believe I fell for that. You guys are real pros. All of you are con artists! A red card. Very clever."

"Okay, now back to your 'guess what' entrance. We give up. So tell us what," Merry said.

"No way. I'm already embarrassed and you'll have another field day making fun of me." She backed away and crossed her arms like a stubborn child. "Changed my mind. I'm not telling."

"Oh, come on. We won't pull your leg anymore. You gotta tell or we'll give you an Indian burn."

"Oh no!" She faked fear, waving her hands in front of her face. "Not an Indian burn!"

Everyone crowded around to administer the wrist-twisting torture if it proved necessary. Silvia raised both hands high over her head. "All right, everybody, back off. In fact, you should sit down for this." She waited until everyone was settled.

"Frank asked me to remarry him." The moment she finished speaking, her friends lept up.

"Whoopee!" Maya called out.

"Good news!" Leonard said.

Merry hugged her. "Oh my!" She hugged her again. "Married. And to your Frank."

"A family reunion!" said Big Eyes.

"It's the Lakota way, coming full circle," Dakotah said. He drew a circle in the air.

"What did the kids say?" Sariah asked.

"They don't know yet. I'm thinking we can surprise them. If you all kick me out in time, maybe we'll do the surprise on Christmas Day."

"Yes, we're kicking you out," Dakotah said. "Already you've been here too long. What was it supposed to be, two months? We want you outta here now! We've pulled everything out of your brain that we need; nothing else in there." Dakotah laughed at his own joke while he checked Silvia's ears and poked his fingers around her brain. "Yep, empty."

"So you're sending me back to D.C. empty-headed?"

"We wanna make certain you blend in with the politicians," Leonard said.

When the laughter settled, sadness swept over Silvia. She would soon be leaving behind what had become a new family of true soulmates. Tears filled her eyes. But before her downer could infect the whole group, Merry changed the mood with her usual practicality.

"So let's see . . . What day is Christmas?" She walked over to the wall calendar. "Okay, good. It's on a weekend. We want you out of here so you and Frank can have a little time for yourselves before the big day. Book your flight, Silvia." She smiled tenderly. "Restart that marriage."

"That's an order!" Dakotah said, making Merry's directive official.

Silvia didn't like goodbyes and was aware she lacked grace when departing. Attempts to hide her emotions resulted in abruptness that left friends and family to wonder if she cared about them. She was determined to do better by her reservation family, all of whom had come to the airport to say goodbye. She tried to give a parting speech; thank them for the sacred honor they had given by sharing their profound values and beautiful souls. Their culture of the spirit showed her what heaven-on-earth would be like when most people were spiritually awakened – like Native Americans. But her words got lost in convulsive sobs and after quick hugs all around, she flew up the boarding ramp. From the plane window she waved and managed a weak smile.

After take-off and her gloom subsided she remembered their promise to stay in tune with each other's lives. She felt good that her teaching duties had been fulfilled. These 'students' had mastered the Divine Mother's knowledge, not just for themselves but for those they taught and then became teachers themselves. But would the suicide rate continue to decline? And as people continued meditating, would the economy and health on the reservation improve? And would she ever see Dakotah and Merry and the others again?

Before she got sucked backed into the blues, a red-haired stewardess in a stylish khaki uniform brought her back to the present with an offer of a blanket and pillow for the five hour flight. Silvia gladly accepted as she hadn't slept the night before what with the contrary emotions rioting through her brain; sorrow to leave her native family yet beyond ecstasy to be with Frank and the children again.

Tenderness flowed from her heart into her throat and eased her face muscles that had stiffened from crying. Even the practical aspects of her renewed life had slid into place. They would live with Frank's mother, who graciously offered to continue helping with the kids so Silvia could work on the cable TV project. John promised there would not be frantic deadlines that required all-nighters and weekends. She would work a normal eight hour day and could join a car pool to get to and from work. There would be plenty of time when she got home to spend with the kids and Frank, do chores, and enjoy a regular family life.

Contentment settled in as she stretched her arms, yawned and curled her body into the tiny space. Her heart flooded with gratitude for the precious gift the Divine Mother gave to humanity. Racism would be purged forever once a critical mass of the world's population took the evolutionary step to became self-realized. Silvia and the thousands world-wide who already practiced the Divine Mother's program were living proof. No way can the attitudes of bigotry and hate survive a cleansing from the almighty spirit.

Abruptly her eyes popped open and she jerked to an upright position. For a moment she thought her life's mission had been fulfilled.

But the thought quickly vanished when she knew she had raced too far ahead of today's reality. How stupid could she be? It would take decades before realization became the norm for the majority and the poison of racism was completely purged.

She laid back down as her body relaxed, just in time to catch a few hours' sleep before landing.

15

’Twas the night before Christmas in the suburbs of Washington, D.C. Frank was busy in his bedroom trying to make it free of dust and clutter. How did she always make everything look so neat? He struggled to tidy up the dresser; then sighed. Only one way to do this. He opened up a large garbage bag, swept everything inside and stuck the bag in a closet. He hung up the clothes that were strewn around; changed the sheets; vacuumed. Then surveyed his work. It wasn't perfect, but he was satisfied. Especially since he knew she would reorganize everything anyway.

Footsteps on the stairs made him quickly shut and lock the door. It was not easy to hide surprises from kids endowed with Sherlock-type sleuth cells running through their brains.

"Frank? "

Thank God, it was his mother. Tessa was in on the surprise. He let her in but quickly shut the door.

"Don't worry. The kids are glued to the TV." She looked around the room. "Hmm. Looks tidy. What did you do with all the clutter?"

He showed her the stuffed bag on the closet floor. She laughed. "Ah. Typical male solution. Here, give it to me, and I'll stash it somewhere downstairs. She'll need room for her shoes, you know. She's a woman."

He was glad his mother had a change of heart toward Silvia, which occurred surprisingly in tandem with his own.

He felt his stomach churn. He'd better hurry. He needed to do some last-minute shopping before Silvia arrived at noon. Everything was timed out to fit *The Plan*. He'd built in leeway for unexpected delays, but only fifteen minutes here or there. The plan included his mother taking the kids to Silvia's mom's by no later than two o'clock. The kids and both grandmothers would spend the night at Helen's and return in the morning. Christmas morning.

He couldn't wait to see the kids' faces. But right now, he couldn't wait to see Silvia.

At the baggage claim, Frank and Silvia's embrace overflowed with feverish passion, typical after a long-distance courtship. Together they shed tears, grateful for the divine intervention that enabled the impossible to become a reality. Then, in concert with the plan, they drove to the local courthouse where the justice of the peace kindly officiated for them on Christmas Eve. By his authority, their remarriage became legal. They had the sanctity they both wanted without having to wait for a formal ceremony.

Once inside the house, they threw off their coats and rushed upstairs to what Frank had labeled the Bridal Suite on a handwritten sign Scotch-taped to the door. Ceremoniously, he scooped Silvia into his arms, who cried and laughed at the same time while he carried her across the threshold.

It was eight o'clock Christmas morning when three kids and two grandmothers clamored through the front door. Frank, in his red-plaid bathrobe, bolted downstairs to greet them. The kids swarmed around the tree, eyed the piles of packages and begged to get on with the traditional Christmas protocol – stockings first, then breakfast, and only after their plates were empty, the long-awaited opening of the presents.

"All right, everybody. Listen up." Frank beckoned them to the bottom of the stairs. "Before we open anything, I have a surprise that will knock your socks off."

The kids looked bewildered at the change in the order of events. Alan eyed his socks with raised eyebrows, causing Frankie to laugh while Linda let her little brother know it was just an expression.

"The surprise is too big to bring down. I had the delivery people put it in place." Frank began to slowly climb the stairs, spreading his arms to keep the kids at bay as they tried to push past.

"It's a new canopy bed for me," Linda said. "I knew it! Just what I wanted!"

"No, it's the electric race-car track we asked for. He set it up in our room!" Frankie said.

"Yippie!" Alan said.

When Frank reached the top stair, he didn't turn left toward the kids' rooms but headed down the long hallway toward his bedroom. The children went silent; too mystified to make a guess. The bedroom door was closed. Frank cringed when he saw his Bridal Suite sign, but yanked it off before the kids noticed. Slowly, slowly he opened the door.

In the middle of the room sat a giant box tied with a big red bow. Everyone gathered around. Alan poked at the box.

"Not big enough for a bed," Linda said.

Frank flicked a switch on the record player. A drum roll sounded.

Frank bent forward; everyone followed his lead.

One arm suddenly pushed out from inside the box. The flaps burst open. Then, like a jack-in-the-box, Silvia sprang up, thrusting both arms into the air. Frank moved in and gracefully, like a choreographed dancer, lifted her out of the box.

Cheers drowned out the drum rolls. They shared hugs, kisses and more hugs.

Frank put his arm around Silvia and announced, "Yesterday your mother and I were re-married. Merry Christmas! Mom's home!

Happy tears rolled down the faces of the grandmothers as they watched the kids cuddle with their parents.

"How come you tricked us?" Frankie asked. He looked annoyed.

"We decided to keep it a surprise Christmas present. What could be better?"

"Well . . . okay. But it shook me up when Mom came out of that box."

Silvia could see the kids were still a bit shocked. "How about we just do our Christmas day like we normally do? You guys ready for that?"

"Well if it's going to be like normal, then you should fix breakfast," Tessa said.

"I'd love to." Silvia had hoped to take over the job. "And the cook never cleans up, so whose turn is it to wash the dishes?"

"Alan's. The youngest always washes the dishes on Christmas Day," Linda said.

Alan screwed up his face. "That's not fair!"

"Not to worry, Alan dear," Grandmother Helen said. "I'm the oldest and the oldest always helps the youngest on Christmas."

"And I get the day off!" Tessa said happily.

"From now on you'll get a lot of days off," Silvia said.

As Christmas music soared through the house, the family inside celebrated the miracle that had brought the Nolan family back to, well, normal.

AFTERWORD

The story just told was inspired by true events. The primary truth is that the Divine Mother actually lived on the earth for 88 years, from 1923 until 2011. Her formal spiritual name is Shri Mataji Nirmala Devi. (Divine Mother is an English translation).

The Divine Mother experienced life as a wife and mother before she became the first and only guru capable of giving self-realization to the masses. She travelled to over 100 countries giving programs just like Silvia experienced in Chapter 7.

Being pragmatic, the Divine Mother developed a simple meditation method to use once the kundalini is activated, to enable the practitioner to heal physically, mentally and emotionally. She named her method Sahaja Yoga; sahaja means born within or natural and yoga means union or yoked to the divine. The kundalini energy is placed in every human's sacrum bone when in the womb, like all other body parts. When the 'owner' has the desire, it can be awakened.

The Divine Mother made certain the ability to awaken kundalini and spread the knowledge of Sahaja Yoga would be shared. It is as simple as passing the light from one candle to enlighten another. She also insisted it be offered to every willing person, regardless of race, creed, nationality, age, status of health or wealth and that it must always, *always* be free of charge. Therefore, Sahaja Yoga Meditation programs, taught by experienced volunteers, can be found in libraries, community rooms and other such venues world-wide and in most major cities in America. On the next page are some links to find more information.

www.shrimataji.org to learn more about the Shri Mataji.

www.sahajayoga.org/worldwidecontacts to find a program near you.

www.simpleself-realization.blog to learn how and why of self-realization.

Black Efforts for Soul in Television was also a real organization which filed a Petition to Deny License Renewal against WMAL-TV in Washington, D.C. for black exclusion. Unity House also was real and inspired the nation-wide avalanche of petitions exposing the lack of black participation in broadcasting and triggered the diversity we see today on television. (See *Ebony Magazine*, November 1970, p.35-44). www.tinyurl.com/y6uj97qs

To contact the author, Carolyn Vance, by e-mail:

carolyn@simpleself-realization.blog

APPRECIATIONS

It Takes A Mother could not have existed without the enlightened wisdom, guidance, and divine love of the Mother of all Mothers, **Shri Mataji Nirmala Devi**.

For teaching me how to love unconditionally goes eternal appreciation to my children, John, Susan, and Jeff and their spouses, Michelle, Russ, and Maribeth, and my grandchildren, Jack, Sami, Alex, Kai, Sean, Logan, Reilly, and Flynn.

Infinite appreciation goes to my parents, Ivan and Elizabeth, and siblings, Joan, Marian, and Roger, who provided a value system that embraces love for all mankind and taught that self-worth comes from taking care of each other.

Deep and heartfelt appreciation goes to my fellow Sahaja Yogis world-wide whose powerful vibrations and brother-sister love, keeps me inspired, healthy and joyful.

To Brian Bell, Sylvia Dooling, and Betty Cooper goes abundant appreciation for taking the time to read and re-read the manuscript and provide useful feedback that greatly improved the quality of *It Takes A Mother*.

To Beth Hill of www.anoveledit.com, www.theeditorsblog.com, and author of *The Magic of Fiction* goes genuine appreciation for her coaching skill to first-time novelists and balanced, professional editing.

To Richard Payment goes lasting appreciation for his generosity in time and skill to transform my manuscript into book sales. Richard is a publisher and editor at Divine Cool Breeze Books and author of *For Want of Wonders* and *Soothsay*.

To my husband, Volodya, goes enduring appreciation for affording me the time, space, and support to attempt to become a writer.

Printed in Great Britain
by Amazon

81325681R00119